DEATH
ON THE
PATH

DAVID
MATTHEWS
DEATH
ON THE
PATH

The Book Guild Ltd

First published in Great Britain in 2022 by
The Book Guild Ltd
Unit E2 Airfield Business Park,
Harrison Road, Market Harborough,
Leicestershire. LE16 7UL
Tel: 0116 2792299
www.bookguild.co.uk
Email: info@bookguild.co.uk
Twitter: @bookguild

Typeset in 11pt Minion Pro

Printed and bound by CPI Group (UK) Ltd, Croydon, CR0 4YY

ISBN 978 1915122 582

British Library Cataloguing in Publication Data.
A catalogue record for this book is available from the British Library.

In fond memory of wonderful family
holidays spent in sixties Cornwall as a child.
David Matthews 2022.

ONE

CUT AND RUN

The white Fiat 500 turned off the A394 after passing through Helston and headed south towards the Cornish coastline. Considering it was still only late October the weather was atrocious. Struggling to see through the torrential rain, Daniel Felton cursed the driving conditions for the umpteenth time. He was not used to this. Having spent the last few years living in a bedsit in West London, he'd had little need for a car. He was now negotiating the narrow approach road that led to his final destination. He was feeling tired, hungry and more than a little anxious, but he'd had little choice in coming down here.

It was close to midnight as he entered the tiny village of Tregarris. According to his cousin Luke, the cottage was tucked away somewhere at the end of the high street. Most of the buildings were in darkness. It vaguely occurred to him that many were probably self-catering establishments that had been shut down for the winter.

After passing through the length of the village, Daniel stopped the car and reached into his pocket for Luke's directions. The cottage was called the Chough apparently, named after the local bird, according to his cousin. He drove on slowly down a dark narrowing lane until he came to a smallish structure set back from the road. Isolated and fully detached from the high street, Daniel reflected that as cottages go, it did not appear the most welcoming. In fact, at that moment, with the incessant rain falling and the shadowy darkness, it looked downright forbidding.

Daniel grabbed his holdall from the passenger seat and made his way to the entrance. He passed a battered wooden sign where he could just make out the name 'Chough' from the faded lettering. Arriving at the door, he pulled a small key from the envelope Luke had given him. It took some time to locate the keyhole, and a few seconds more before he managed to turn the key in the stiffened lock.

The door opened into a dark interior. For a brief moment Daniel fought an impulse to return to the relative comfort of the Fiat. Stepping over the threshold into the small hallway, his overall impression was of a building that was unloved and abandoned. Luke had not been joking when he had said that the cottage needed some TLC. The hallway smelt of a damp mustiness. He felt for the light switch along the wall. Much to his relief a dim light illuminated the rest of the ground floor. At least the electric was working. A large grandfather clock stood isolated on one side; he noticed the hands had stopped at three o'clock. Closing the front door behind him, he entered the first room to his left. Switching on the light, he was disappointed to see that the only item of furniture in what he assumed to be the living area was a sofa. What did please him was that it appeared to be quite new. It looked like his cousin had at least made a start in civilising his new investment. He made his way to the small kitchen area on the opposite side of the hallway. A kettle, a new-looking freestanding oven and a small fridge was the sum total of equipment. A tiny sink area overlooked a window at the front of the house. He was not surprised to discover that the fridge was empty. Opening a cupboard under the sink, he was relieved to find some crockery and a selection of pots and pans. A small drawer contained some cutlery. He gave a small cheer when he found a few teabags left in a tin. He was grateful for small mercies. Making a conscious effort to control his underlying anxiety, he slowly mounted the small flight of stairs that led to the upper floor. Once at the top, and after some further cautious investigation, he discovered two empty bedrooms. There was some neatly folded bedlinen placed on one of the bare floors.

Moving further along the narrow landing, he was heartened to discover a small, newly installed shower room. His cousin Luke had purchased the cottage with a view to renting it out as a self-catering holiday home. Obviously there was still a lot of work to be done, but he appeared to be making some progress. Daniel went back downstairs and made himself a cup of tea. He warmed his hands on the mug as he sat on the sofa lost in thought. Despite the fact that there were only a few home comforts, he felt extremely grateful to his cousin. He had left London in a hurry. His cousin had provided this bolthole. Luke really was more like a brother to him – he was definitely his best friend. They had always been close from childhood. He could not remember a time when he had not been around. Certainly he was the only person he could have told about his addiction. He looked around the empty room. How had it come to this? Aged twenty-five and alone here in the middle of nowhere. No prospects, no self-esteem and no Lauren. She would be worried about him, but she would get over it. He was not worthy of her. He reassured himself that she would be happier without him.

He struggled to put an exact date on when his internet gambling had begun to take him over. It had all started with a few horseraces and some football scores. Looking back it had all been so damn convenient: at his bedsit alone in Marylebone with a laptop, totally engrossed. It had seemed to lure him in imperceptibly, until eventually his moods and personality became ruled by its accessibility. He could not remember exactly when it was that he lost interest in everything else but the gambling. His telesales job at the call centre had become even more mind-numbing – just a means to an end in financing his addiction. Inevitably the debts began to grow. Over time he gradually became submerged in a dark world of payday loans, overdrafts, loan sharks and debt collectors. In recent weeks he had begun to feel completely overwhelmed, totally losing track of his finances. Increasingly he had begun to feel that the only answer was to run away from everything and everyone.

That difficult choice was made for him just a couple of days ago when two menacing individuals turned up at his bedsit. They gave him the distinct impression that if he did not settle his account pretty soon there would be painful consequences for him. Severely shaken, he had felt too ashamed to tell Lauren. He knew that she would probably have had a suspicion that something had been wrong for some time, but she would have had no idea of the scale of the problem. So, frightened and desperate, he had gone to his cousin. Luke had always been good with money. He even remembered him buying and selling for profit in the school playground. It was no surprise that he was now a successful estate agent who was building up a lucrative property portfolio. For all his recent problems he would never have dreamt of asking Luke for money as he knew he could never pay it back. He valued their friendship too much to ever risk it in such a shaming way. He knew that his cousin had been shocked that he had got himself in such a mess, and angry that he had not gone to him sooner. But, typically, Luke had forgiven him and was soon putting together a practical plan to give him some breathing space. It was his suggestion Daniel should lie low in his Cornish property for a week or so, while also insisting he help with his rent arrears.

Daniel thought back to the expression on his landlord's face when he told him he was going away for a few days and handed him the folded wedge of notes: a combination of delighted surprise and cynical suspicion. He had already walked away from his boring job the previous day. He would not be going back there. Despite his protests, Luke had also given him some spending money and the use of one of his company cars to get down to Cornwall. There was only one condition that his cousin had demanded. That he hand over his laptop and smartphone and switch to a basic, non-internet mobile. It had been a no-brainer. He could not risk any temptation. Daniel took a last swig of his tea and put the mug down. The cottage still felt creepily silent. Deciding to keep the lights on, he curled up on the sofa and fell into an exhausted sleep.

*

Daniel woke up with a start. For a moment he felt he was falling. Then he remembered he had fallen asleep on the sofa and was perched precariously on the edge. He sat up and rubbed his eyes. The morning sun was shining brightly through the living-room window. He stood up and slowly stretched, easing the stiffness out of his awakening limbs. He walked over to the window. With the bright sunlight in the blue sky and the boisterous crying of the seagulls, it all felt and looked more cheerful than his earlier rain-soaked arrival. His mobile phone told him it was quarter past nine but was displaying no service. Luke had told him that the reception was poor in the area. He'd had a good sleep: probably the best he'd had for some time.

He went over to his holdall and pulled out a towel and some toiletries. He suddenly remembered the new shower upstairs and thought, with some anticipation, that it was a good time to try it out. It did not disappoint. After the long drive and fixed sleeping position on the sofa, it felt fantastic to be doused in the powerful jets of steaming hot water. After taking his time, he finally stepped out of the cubicle and towelled himself. He had left in such a rush that there had only been time to pack a few clothing items. He changed his shirt and pants; his socks would have to do another day.

He opened the front door and the fresh gust of autumnal air reminded him of how ravenously hungry he was. Taking a step outdoors, his attention was drawn to the large cast-iron doorbell which hung outside. He had failed to notice it when he had arrived in the dark last night. He could not resist pulling on the tattered leather strap. It made a satisfyingly loud peal that seemed to echo across the cliff tops. Looking across to the sea, he was surprised how close the cottage was to the coastal path. Quickly putting on his parka and making sure he had the door key, he left to walk down to the village in search of some sustenance. It was a Monday morning and the village high street was bathed in sunlight. The few people that passed him in the street seemed to glance at him curiously but looked cheerful enough. It appeared that an unfamiliar face out of the holiday season in Tregarris did not go unnoticed. Halfway along the street he passed an attractive-looking pub called the Jolly Pirate. From what he could see of the food menu and the bar area through the front windows, it looked worth a visit.

At the end of the street he was comforted to discover a well-stocked convenience store and he was soon returning to the cottage with a bag full of foodstuffs. Having a clearer view of the Chough in the morning sun, he was able to get a better look at the cottage as he approached. Small and compact, with the bright sunlight gleaming on its whitewashed walls, it was not an unpleasant sight.

Half an hour later he was finishing off a plate of bacon and eggs washed down with a cup of tea. It was always one of his favourites, but he seldom remembered it tasting better. Sitting back on the sofa he noticed his phone had a missed call. It looked like the single bar of reception had allowed a call to get through. He recognised Luke's number and noticed he had left a voicemail. He went outside the front door to see if he could get a better reception, but the no signal message stubbornly remained. He remembered Luke mentioning that the more you went inland the stronger the signal.

Fifteen minutes later he was seated in the Fiat 500 heading for the Helston Road. He pulled over to the side of the A394 about a mile from Helston and left the car. It was strangely comforting to hear his cousin's voicemail.

'Hello, you old scallywag, hope you got there alright. Give us a call on this number as soon as you get a signal. By the way, you will be getting a bed delivered this afternoon so don't stray too far.'

Daniel was pleased to hear about the delivery; he did not fancy another night on the sofa. He rang Luke's number and covered up his other ear as a car hurtled past. It rang three times before Luke answered.

'Hi, Daniel. How are you getting on?'

'I'm doing OK. It all seems a little surreal if I'm honest.'

'It's bound to feel a bit strange at first, but the idea is that you can forget about everything and just chill. What do you think of the cottage?'

'It seemed a little bit creepy when I arrived, but it looked good in the sunshine this morning. Just a little sparse on the amenities, though.'

'Sorry about that, I am working on it. After a coat of paint in every room and some new carpets it will be transformed by next summer. Not tempted to make a start on the painting while you're there?'

'No, thanks.'

'I thought I'd ask, just in case you were tempted to release your inner Picasso.'

Daniel was relieved to hear he was joking. 'Very funny.'

'I take it you don't want me to say anything to Aunt Alice and Uncle Bob?'

Daniel had forgotten about his parents. They would be mortified if they found out. With a slight catch in his throat he replied, 'The less they know the better.' The thought of his parents brought home the reality of his situation. 'I really can't believe the mess I've made of my life, Luke.'

'Now don't start feeling sorry for yourself. This is just a phase you're going through. We'll soon get you on your feet again.' Thinking of something to cheer him up, Luke added, 'I can recommend the beer in the Jolly Pirate.'

Daniel thought back to the cheerful-looking pub. 'Yes, I've clocked that already, I'll give it a go.'

'Do you want Kate to have a word with Lauren? Tell her that you're OK?'

'Is there any point? She'd be far better off without me.'

'As you are at the moment that's true, but she will still be worried just the same.'

Daniel hesitated for a moment. 'I suppose so.'

'You know it makes sense. I'll be coming down to see you on Friday night around seven.'

'Thanks, mate, I really don't deserve you.'

'True, but someone has to sort you out. Watch out for the bed delivery. Be sure to let me know of anything you need.'

'I could do with some extra socks and pants.'

'Consider it done. See you on Friday. We can talk about a plan going forward.'

'OK. Cheers,' Daniel replied dubiously.

The line went dead and Daniel returned to the Fiat to head back to the cottage. Much as he appreciated Luke's good intentions, in that moment he had serious doubts if anything could be done to dig him out of the self-inflicted hellhole he had dug himself.

*

After the phone call with Daniel, Luke Sadler sat at his office desk in Hoxton looking thoughtful. He was still feeling angry that Daniel had not come to him sooner. His cousin at times had always been a little too easy-going in his approach to life, but he had been genuinely shocked and concerned when Daniel had confessed the extent of his gambling problem. He would never have seen that coming. The first person he had thought of was his girlfriend Lauren. They were supposed to be saving up for a place to move in together.

He rose and walked over to the other side of the office where Kate was sitting.

His bride-to-be was holding the phone to her ear but not talking. She looked at him and smiled. 'It's alright. I've been put on hold.'

Luke could just hear the faint notes of *The Four Seasons* by Vivaldi coming from her phone.

'I've just spoken to Daniel, he sounds OK.'

Kate's first concern was for her friend. 'Has he spoken to Lauren?'

Luke shook his head. 'Not yet. He wants you to tell her not to worry.'

'Where is the shit bag? Is he with someone else?'

Luke put his hands up. 'Believe me, it's nothing like that.'

Kate looked irritated. 'I wish you would tell me what's going on!'

Luke adopted a soothing tone. 'All in good time, hun, all in good time. Believe me, it's extremely delicate.'

Kate pulled a face. 'I will ring her this afternoon. But you had better tell me tonight.'

'I will, hun. Thanks.'

He went back to his desk. He could understand Kate's concern for her friend. When he first started going out with Kate she had worked with Lauren at Selfridges in Oxford Street. They went back a long way. It had been Kate that had introduced her to Daniel. Luke shook his head. What a mess! He could not begin to imagine what it felt like to be in Daniel's position. Money had never been a problem to him. He had always found it easy to make a profit. Buying low and selling high was second nature to him. Leaving school at seventeen and getting a job with an estate agent, he had ridden the wave of the property boom in London. Shrewd judgement and an instinctive nose for the market had now led to him having two branches of Sadler's offices in fashionable Hoxton. How much of it was down to luck he had no way of knowing. He had never experienced the downside. His thoughts turned back to his cousin. How to help Daniel?

*

It was mid-afternoon as Daniel closed his eyes and drifted to the gentle soundtrack of distant surf and crying seagull. The new bed felt good; the contours of the mattress seemed to yield comfortably with his body shape. The delivery men had been a touch sullen but impressively efficient, as they manoeuvred the mattress upstairs with practised expertise. He could not recall the last time he had felt so relaxed.

His thoughts began to turn slowly to his financial plight. He really had no idea how much he owed in total, but he was sure it was not much short of ten grand. He thought of the two men who had put the frighteners on him. They had not revealed exactly who they were collecting for, but they had left him in no doubt that it was someone pretty ruthless. He thought back to all the people he had borrowed from in the last few months. Besides the odd money lender and friends and acquaintances, he could only recall being approached by a smart-looking chap who got talking to him while drinking in his favourite local, the Royal Oak in York Street. Aged somewhere in his mid-thirties, he remembered him being particularly sociable and friendly. After having an enjoyable discussion about Premiership football, he recalled that the conversation had been guided towards finance suspiciously quickly. He realised now that he must have been identified as someone to be targeted because of his cashflow problems. Somehow they had found out about his history of failed credit arrangements beforehand. It had obviously been no chance meeting. What a fool he had been to take up the man's offer of unlimited funds. The gambling addiction had obviously addled his brain. He could not remember exactly how much he had borrowed, but it was certainly nowhere near the amount the two men were demanding. Starting to feel agitated, he sat up on the bed and put his head in his hands. He felt he needed some fresh air.

Leaving the cottage, Daniel made the short walk to the coastal path. He stood for a while watching the foaming white waves chasing each other to the rocky shoreline. In that moment he wished Lauren was standing there next to him. He was starting to miss her. He breathed in the ozone. He almost felt dizzy. It was certainly nothing like the usual Marylebone smog he was forced to inhale. He looked both to his left and right: both vistas looked attractive. He chose to go right. He walked in that direction for about an hour and in that time he only saw two people. He had visited Cornwall before, but on a day like this, he could not remember it looking so stunning. At one stage he actually forgot all about his woes and felt the beginnings of a feel-good factor. That hadn't happened for a while. Though he knew he would have to face up to his problems eventually, Luke's suggestion he came down here for some breathing space seemed a good one.

Retracing his steps, he headed back along the path towards the cottage. About a mile along, a shambolic-looking figure emerged in front of him. It was a man and he did not look a healthy specimen. Unkempt and unshaven, he wore a grubby-looking trench coat tied with string at the waist. On his back he carried a bright red rucksack with what looked like a small banjo attached. As Daniel drew near, the man scowled and cursed at him. He was not friendly. As far as Daniel could make out, he thought he detected a Scottish accent as the man continued to swear and slur at him. Daniel was glad to leave him behind, but he did glance over his shoulder a few times to make sure he was not following. *Poor sod*, he thought. *I wonder what his hard-luck story consisted of?* He shook his head and muttered to himself, 'I guess you can always find someone worse off than yourself if you look hard enough.'

*

Luke took another long sip of his Cabernet-Shiraz as he looked at Kate. They had just finished their Thai takeaway and Kate was putting on the coffee. The conversation about Daniel was not one he was looking forward to, but the time had come to tell all. They had returned from work and were in their house that bordered Victoria Park in Hackney. Back in the reign of Queen Victoria, it had originally been built alongside a row of similarly large houses for the comfortably off. Throughout the twentieth century the buildings had gradually lost their appeal and splendour. Since the millennium, however, they had become valuable and fashionable once again in the London property boom. Mainly this had been due to the unexpected gentrification of the more unfashionable boroughs of London in the noughties. Young middle-class professionals in finance, media and the art world had moved in and made them trendy. Working in the property market, Luke had been in the forefront of this development. He had been in the right place at the right time and had taken full advantage. He moved over to the sofa as Kate handed him a mug of coffee and joined him. After two years of some serious investment in the house, it was now a comfortable mix of modern tech and late Victorian splendour.

Kate looked at him expectantly.

Luke shuffled a little uncomfortably. 'How was Lauren?'

Kate thought back to the distressing phone conversation she had with her friend. 'Not good. She sounded very upset.'

'Understandable. Believe me, there is a good reason for Daniel's disappearance and it has got nothing to do with his feelings for her.'

Kate looked exasperated. 'What is going on?'

Luke took a deep breath. 'It's like this. Somehow, without anyone knowing, Daniel has developed an online gambling addiction.'

'What!' Kate was poleaxed.

Luke went on. 'It's a really serious situation. It seems the idiot has spent most of his spare time locked away in his bedsit with his laptop for company. So much so that he now has debts coming out of his ears. Some of them to some pretty unsavoury characters by the sound of it. Surely Lauren must have suspected something was wrong?'

Kate managed to splutter out an answer. 'She said she had seen less of him in recent weeks. To the point that she was beginning to wonder if he was seeing someone else. He'd told her he'd been busy with work.'

'He was certainly working alright, digging himself into one great big hole. He phoned me late afternoon on Friday. He sounded pretty desperate, asked me if I could meet him at Liverpool Street Station outside McDonald's. It turns out that two big blokes had turned up at the bedsit and threatened him with menaces if he didn't cough up some dosh.'

Kate was incredulous. 'What! He was blowing all of his salary on gambling?'

'It looks like it. At least that won't be happening again because he's now walked out on his job.'

Kate thought once more of her friend. 'Lauren has been saving up for a flat. The idea was that he was doing the same.'

'I think you can put that one on the backburner. We have seriously got to sort him out first.'

'Where is he now?'

'I have packed him off to the little cottage we purchased down in Cornwall. Give him some breathing space. I lent him the Fiat.'

'When was this?'

'Sunday night.'

'I take it you were going to tell me eventually.'

Luke took her hand. 'Of course I was, hun. Daniel didn't want Lauren to know anything about his addiction. It had to be at the right time.'

'So, what happens now?'

'I'm going down to see him on Friday night. Sort out a plan of action.'

'When does Lauren get to know?'

'Simple. When it looks like Daniel's getting back on his feet.' Luke looked at her pleadingly. 'I really need your support on this one, Kate.'

There was a pause as Kate let out a deep sigh. 'OK.'

Luke looked relieved. 'Thanks, hun.'

*

Daniel could not help feeling a slight twinge of anxiety as he paused briefly at the door of the Jolly Pirate. He knew that his solitary attendance would be bound to draw attention in such a tight-knit community. Feeling more than a little self-conscious, he kept his eyes straight ahead as he walked to the bar. He was quickly put at his ease by the landlord's pleasant countenance and genial manner.

'Good evening young, sir. What will you be having?'

Daniel studied the tap beers on display. There appeared to be a good selection. He finally narrowed it down to the Proper Job or Tribute, from the St Austell Brewery; he decided on the latter.

'Good choice, though you can't go wrong with any of these, to be fair.'

Daniel felt the publican was giving him a good appraisal as he pulled the pint.

'Are you staying in the village?'

'For a few days.'

He handed over the pint. 'Enjoy.'

Daniel took a long swill of his foaming pint. It hit the spot. He raised his glass. 'Cheers.'

The landlord looked pleased. 'Where are you staying?'

'The Chough cottage.'

'Old Tom's place?' He sounded surprised. 'Didn't think it was very hospitable just now.'

'My cousin has recently purchased it. He plans to have it ready for next summer.'

Daniel became aware of a fellow customer along the bar taking a keen interest in the conversation. He looked like one of the locals but seemed friendly enough.

The man grinned at him. 'Not another Emmet from up north – we can't even get a rest from them out of season.'

Daniel guessed that the word Emmet was probably a Cornish expression for holidaymaker, but it amused him that he was being described as from up north.

The owner behind the bar winked at Daniel. 'Sid thinks anyone further up than the River Tamar is a northerner, take no notice.'

Daniel was curious. 'Doesn't the village do well out of the tourists?'

The man looked pointedly at the landlord. 'There's some that do and some that don't, depending on their circumstances. That's all I'm saying.'

The landlord laughed. 'You would soon miss having something to moan about if all the Emmets stayed away.'

The man's expression was still genial, but he poked his finger on the bar as he made his point. 'At least there would be more homes for the locals.'

Daniel could sense an underlying seriousness beneath the banter. Seeing that the man's glass was almost empty, he thought it would be a good gesture if he offered him a refill.

Sid looked a bit surprised. 'No, it's alright, me luvver, another time.' With that he drained his glass and waved to a couple of the other customers before leaving the pub.

The publican looked a touch apologetic. 'Don't mind Sid. He's just a touch conflicted regarding the tourist trade. One day he's for it, another he's against. He was the same with Brexit. There's no harm in him.'

Daniel gave a polite smile before leaving the bar and taking a seat. He looked around the pub. A warming log fire dominated one end of the bar area. At the far end he could see an arched entrance to a cosy-looking dining room. A pair of cutlasses and a variety of horse brasses adorned the brickwork on the walls. He noticed two elderly gents sitting together at a round table. Both bearded and ruddy of complexion, he thought they blended perfectly with their surroundings. From time to time he caught their eye and they seemed to be regarding him with amused interest. He felt relaxed. The change of scene had taken off all the pressure and misery he had been feeling. So much so that he had not once experienced any urge to gamble. It was as if his recent life in London had belonged to someone else. He felt detached. The only thing he was missing was Lauren.

Two hours later he was still sitting there, swilling his fourth pint of Tribute. The pub had become busier as it filled up with the regular clientele. They all seemed to be on first-name terms with the landlord, whose name apparently was Reg. One end of the bar had got a lot noisier, as some of the local young men had entered and were letting off some steam. In particular, he noticed a tall fair-haired fella amongst the company that seemed to be occasionally staring at him with what he detected to be a hint of hostility. At one point earlier on in the evening he had squeezed past this particular individual to go to the toilet. He had been aware of a slight shoulder bump at the time. Casting his mind back to the incident, he wasn't really sure if it had not been intentional. Looking across to the two old men at the round table, he could not help noticing that in front of the remaining empty chair, a full pint of beer stood untouched. It was as if they were expecting someone to arrive. The untouched pint was still there half an hour later when he got up to leave.

Walking down the narrow, dark lane that led to the cottage, the combination of the four pints of beer and the cold sea air had made him feel a touch heady. As he neared the Chough he began to wish that he had brought a torch with him. In the inky-black darkness, the cottage had again appeared to take on the more sinister image of the night before. Nearing the gated entrance he was suddenly startled by a hostile-sounding voice.

'Bleddy Tuss.'

He peered in the direction of the shout. It seemed to have come from a raised set of bushes about thirty metres to his left. The only thing he could hear was the sound of the coastal breeze as he looked into the blackness. It was certainly the first time he had ever heard the word 'Tuss'. He had the distinct impression that it was definitely not meant as a term of endearment. Walking quickly to the door and fishing for the key, he heard the shout again. It sounded very aggressive. He wasted no further time in getting inside the cottage.

TWO

A BODY AND A BELL

D aniel was having a restive night. Disappointingly, he was really finding it difficult to appreciate the new bed. He had been unsettled by the abusive voice in the bush. Tossing and turning as he tried to relax, his mind had become overactive. At one stage he thought he had heard distant voices outside, softly floating over the faint sound of the surf. Eventually he sank into a fitful sleep.

He woke with a jolt. Had he heard the bell outside or had it been a part of his dream? Something had woken him up. He lay there in silence. Then he heard it again. This time there was no doubt. Someone was outside ringing the cast-iron bell. He reached for his mobile and looked at the time. It was three o'clock. Who the devil would be ringing at that time? He rose from the bed and went to the front window. He slowly pulled the curtain to one side. His view of the doorway from the upstairs window was partially obscured, but there appeared to be nothing to see other than the pitch-black exterior. He stood there watching for a few minutes. Whoever it was had appeared to have gone. He returned to his bed. For the next hour he lay on the bed with his eyes open, at any moment expecting the bell to burst into life once more. It was to be some time before nature finally kicked in and he sank into merciful slumber.

*

Luke sat lost in thought as the tube train rattled along the circle line towards Baker Street. It was Tuesday morning and he was on his way to Daniel's bedsit in York Street. He had decided to have the day off work in order to have a meeting with the landlord. He was pretty sure that once Daniel returned and collected his possessions, there would be no way he would still want to live there. Also, if he was being honest with himself, he did not want him to either. If Daniel was to move on in his life, he needed to make a fresh start.

The train pulled in to Baker Street and Luke took a swig from his bottle of water before leaving the carriage. The address was a first-floor flat in a townhouse that had been converted into four small bedsits. In his job as an estate agent it was an arrangement he was well familiar with. A brass unit was fixed to the wall which displayed four names with buttons alongside and a small camera. Luke pressed the appropriate button for Daniel. He had arranged to meet the landlord in Daniel's room. After a few seconds the buzzer sounded and he heard the latch on the door disengage. He climbed the carpeted stairs to Daniel's room. When he reached the landing, the landlord was standing there to greet him.

Luke held out his hand. 'Good morning, Mr Ashley. I much appreciate your time; this shouldn't take too long.'

Taking Luke's hand, he answered, 'I am glad to hear it. Time is money, after all, Mr Sadler.'

They moved into Daniel's room and closed the door.

Mr Ashley went on, 'Where is your cousin? Hope he is keeping out of trouble.'

Luke did not want to give too much away. 'He's having a break; I think he needed it.'

'It doesn't surprise me. I was not the only person he owed money to, not by a long chalk. These last few months there have been all sorts coming here. I've tried to cut him as much slack as I could, I really have.'

'I'm sure you have, Mr Ashley, and I would like to apologise on Daniel's behalf.'

'I have known him a long while, I liked the boy.'

'He has always said you were fair.'

'He was as good as gold in the first year, but this last one it's been like trying to get blood out of a stone.'

'Well, you'll be glad to know that we are sorting him out now.'

'Is he coming back?'

'I very much doubt it, Mr Ashley. He'll be able to say goodbye when he collects his things. By the way, I would appreciate you not giving out too much information if anyone comes asking.'

Ashley touched his nose. 'Mum's the word, Mr Sadler, I won't pry as to what's got him into trouble. Just tell him I wish him well.'

'I will. Now how much does he still owe you?'

Mr Ashley took a small notebook from his pocket.

'Well, he made a payment just before he disappeared, so his account is looking healthier than it has for some time. I would say one hundred and seventy.'

Luke took out his cheque book. 'I would also like you to hold the room for a couple of weeks, so is it alright if I also pay you for two weeks in advance?'

Mr Ashley looked delighted. 'No problem.'

After writing out the cheque, and handing it over, Luke pointed to the wardrobe. 'I just want to take a few of Daniel's clothes if that's OK?'

'Sure, I'll leave you to it.'

Luke quickly tossed some socks and pants into a Tesco bag he found in a cupboard before finally leaving the room.

Exiting on to the street, Luke noticed a man who seemed to be loitering on the pavement outside. They glanced at each other briefly. After walking some way down the street, Luke glanced back at him. The man seemed to be looking up at the flat. He took a mental note of his appearance: middle-aged, medium height and not the most elegant sartorially. In fact, a little bit shabby. Luke suspected that it was just possible he was looking for Daniel. He turned and made his way to the Baker Street tube station.

*

Daniel had woken up to a damp and misty morning. In truth, he did not feel too good. A combination of a disturbed sleep, the voice in the bush and a bell in the night, had left him feeling anxious and depressed. After getting washed and dressed he planned to have a morning stroll along the coastal path in the hope of lifting his spirits.

Stepping outside the cottage, he could not help glancing at the tattered strap hanging from the bell. Swinging gently in the breeze, he wondered who would have given it a tug at such an ungodly hour. Looking at the poor visibility on the coastal path, he decided to change his plan and have a drive into Helston. As he approached the Fiat, he noticed a long, deeply etched line along the length of the car. It looked like it had been keyed. This was getting personal. It was beginning to look like someone really did not want him around. Swearing under his breath, he sighed heavily before getting in the car and driving away.

*

Sarah Thomson was enjoying her late morning constitutional along the coastal path. Though it was misty, she enjoyed the path in all its moods. This was something she loved to do ever since she had first moved to Tregarris some six years ago. It was as much a part of her daily routine as cleaning her teeth. Seeing the roof of old Tom's cottage in the distance, she knew she was nearing the end of her walk. She missed old Tom; he had been a real character. It must have been all of two years now since he had died. She had never known his wife. As she understood it, Tom had been widowed for the best part of ten years.

When she had passed the Chough cottage earlier that morning, she had been a little surprised to see a car parked outside. She wondered who the new inhabitant could be. One thing for sure: it would not be too long before she would find out. News travelled fast in Tregarris. Looking out to the horizon, she could see that the mist was just beginning to lift. Nearing the turn that took her back to the village, something caught her attention just a few yards ahead. At first, she thought indignantly, that it was an old sack that had been dumped on the side of the path. But as she drew nearer, she realised with a quickening pulse that it was the body of a man. He was lying on his side facing the hedge and away from the path. It did not take her long to realise that it was the body of a man who was obviously dead.

*

Sergeant Jack Wilkins from the Devon and Cornwall County Police had been just about to bite into his early lunchtime sandwich, when the call had come in. He had wasted little time in getting to Tregarris from the Godolphin Road police station in Helston. Inside the roped-off area where the body was found, two crime scene examiners were already busy laying out their grid patterns and taking photographs of the corpse.

'So walking the coastal path is a regular part of your routine, Miss Thomson?'

Miss Thomson was still a little flushed with adrenaline. 'Pretty much every day, unless I'm staying at my sister's in Penzance.'

'So you were saying that you are sure he is someone you have seen before?'

'Definitely. I saw him only yesterday. He was swearing and cursing as he usually did.'

The sergeant noticed that there was a murmur of agreement and a nodding of heads in the gathering crowd.

One of the bystanders joined in. 'He's been seen up and down the path for the last two months. Miserable beggar he was too, never a good word to say to anyone.'

The sergeant turned back to Miss Thomson, who had raised her hand to speak. 'Something you'd like to add, Miss Thomson?'

'He usually carried a bright red rucksack on his back, with a banjo.'

The bystander butted in once again. 'No one's ever heard him play a note with it, though. Not even a Scottish ditty.'

Sergeant Wilkins was interested. 'So you think he was Scottish then?'

There was no hesitation from the bystander. 'He had a thick Glaswegian accent.'

They all moved to one side as the ambulance arrived. This was immediately followed by another vehicle carrying the doctor. Wilkins immediately recognised Doctor Harrington. He was the usual local GP the police called in for these situations.

The doc looked a bit flustered. 'Sorry I'm late, Officer; got a bit tied up in surgery.'

'That's OK, Doc. Looks like natural causes but will be interested to hear your opinion.'

The doctor nodded before walking towards the roped-off area. A couple of other officers appeared.

Wilkins was glad to see them. A small crowd had begun to congregate as the news of the body spread. 'Would appreciate if you can disperse this crowd – it seems to be growing by the minute.'

There were a few moans as the locals were moved on. They had been enjoying the novelty of the occasion. Wilkins looked around him. His eyes rested on the Chough cottage.

He turned to Miss Thomson. 'Do you know if there is anyone living in the cottage at the moment?'

'It's been empty for a couple of years since old Tom passed away, though funnily enough there was a white car outside this morning. It seems to have gone now.'

Wilkins looked at the close proximity of the cottage to the body site. 'It's probably not significant.' He heard the sound of a car coming up the lane behind him. He turned to look at it and uttered, 'But then again.' It was Daniel returning in the white Fiat.

*

Daniel was humming along to a Brandon Flowers CD as he drove back from Helston. He had felt so down in the dumps when he had arrived there earlier that morning. So much so, that he had been sorely tempted to ring Lauren but had eventually decided against it. What was the point? He was bad news for Lauren. What right did he have to inflict his miserable existence on her?

After parking the car he had meandered around the Helston streets aimlessly looking into shop windows, most of the time totally oblivious to what he was seeing.

He eventually began to feel a little better after purchasing a couple of new shirts and treating himself to some fish and chips in Coinagehall Street. Now driving through the Tregarris High Street, he was looking forward to getting back to the cottage and making himself a pot of tea. The first clue he had that there was something amiss was the amount of people milling around. At one point he had to slow the car at the top of the lane to avoid the people returning from the coastal path. It occurred to him that perhaps there had been an exciting event like a dramatic sea rescue or an entertaining air show.

What he did not expect to see was an ambulance and three police cars when he rounded the bend that led to the cottage. As he got out of the car a policeman approached him. 'Good afternoon, sir, we have a little incident going on at the minute. A man has been found dead on the coastal path.'

Daniel was taken aback. 'Christ, poor man.'

Sergeant Wilkins glanced at the cottage. 'You are staying here, sir?'

'Yes.'

'Holidaymaker?'

'Kind of.' There was a silence and Daniel sensed the officer wanted a little more information. 'I decided to take a break from London, getting away for a bit. The cottage belongs to my cousin.'

Wilkins took out his notepad. 'Can I have your name, sir?'

'Daniel, Daniel Felton.'

'What's the name of your cousin?'

'Luke Sadler.'

Wilkins shut his notebook. 'It's looking like the poor fellow collapsed, but you don't mind if I ask you a couple of questions?'

'No problem.'

'Did you happen to hear or see anything unusual last night, Mr Felton?'

Daniel thought of the bell and the voice in the bush but felt this was not the right time to complicate things and draw unwarranted attention. 'Nothing comes to mind. Do you know who he is?'

'From what we have gathered so far it seems a fair bet he was a bit of a drifter. The doc is examining him at the moment so we should soon find out a little more.'

Thinking of the abusive Scot he had encountered the previous day, Daniel said, 'I suppose there are quite a lot of wanderers that use the path.'

'A fair few. Mind you, they are not all known for carrying a banjo on their back.'

Daniel could not help giving a start. 'I saw him yesterday afternoon. He had a Scottish accent. He was very abusive. I felt sorry for him.'

'Yes, Mr Felton, life can be very harsh for some.' Wilkins studied Daniel's face keenly. 'You will be sticking around for a while, Mr Felton?'

'That's the plan.' Daniel turned towards the cottage. He felt he needed that cup of tea.

Wilkins turned to one of the officers. 'Can you two take a look along the coastal path, east and west? We are looking for a red rucksack and a banjo.'

The two officers nodded and walked off in the direction of the path.

A few minutes after Daniel's departure, the doc returned from giving the body a preliminary examination.

Sergeant Wilkins was interested to hear the doc's first impressions. 'What do you think, Doc?'

The doc shook his head. 'He's a poor specimen. Could be a heart attack brought on by exposure. Looking at him it was going to happen sooner rather than later.' The doc still looked pensive.

Wilkins asked, 'Something on your mind, Doc?'

'There were two small sores on his neck. Looked like cigarette burns. Probably nothing to do with his death, but as it stands I cannot one hundred per cent rule out foul play. We need a PM on this one, Sergeant.'

'You've got it, Doc.'

The doctor returned to his car and was followed a few seconds later by two ambulance men carrying a stretcher. They were transporting the body to the Royal Cornwall Hospital near Truro.

Wilkins watched the ambulance drive off. From what the doctor had said there was a small chance that the death was not as straightforward as at first seemed. He glanced reflectively over to the Chough cottage. Then there was Daniel Felton. There was something odd, but he couldn't put his finger on it. He seemed a nice enough chap. But a solitary young man, down from London, staying in this remote cottage out of season? What exactly was he getting away from?

*

'So it looks like he has definitely left the area?' Joe

Blades was sitting behind a small desk in his makeshift office in Beak Street, Soho. He was not a happy man. There were zero chances of him getting his money back if the debtor had disappeared. In this case the debtor, Daniel Felton, had appeared to have done exactly that. Across the desk from him was Private Investigator Mark Reid. He had not long returned from Daniel's bedsit.

'It certainly looks like it. His landlord said he had paid up some of his rent on the Sunday evening unexpectedly, before saying he was going away for a while.'

Blades looked both surprised and suspicious. 'How could he do that? Why would he do that? He promised me he would pay back all he owed next week.'

'From what the landlord told me, he had also been surprised. He had been putting no great pressure on Felton to pay up his rent.'

Blades smelled a rat. 'So why did he not choose to pay me the money? He must be getting the wrong advice from somewhere.'

Mark Reid thought he knew the answer to that one. 'My guess is it's the cousin. I caught a glimpse of him when he was leaving the house. I thought it was Daniel at first. They have a slightly different colouring but there is definitely a resemblance.'

'Do we have a name?'

'That's a good question. I did ask the landlord for the cousin's name, but he clammed up as if he felt he had revealed too much already.'

Blades rubbed his chin reflectively. 'OK, Mr Reid, leave it with me. I will get back to you when I have some further information.'

Mark Reid left the tiny apartment block that doubled as Mr Blade's office and turned towards Regent Street. He had taken an instant dislike to Joe Blades, and he suspected the man was not all he made himself out to be; but in his line of work it was sometimes best not to ask too many questions.

Back in the office, Joe Blades picked up the telephone. He needed the name of the cousin. This looked like a job for Vince and Max. He dialled the number.

*

Detective Inspector Martin Everett entered the office in his usual loud and grandiose manner. Sergeant Wilkins and PC Sandra Kent exchanged tolerant glances and kept their heads down. They were seated in their first-floor office in Godolphin Road, Helston. The police station spread across three levels, with the cells being on the lower floor, the reporting desk and interview room at ground level, with a small open-plan office on the first. Everett had just returned from a strategic development meeting in Exeter, and he was complaining that it had been a complete waste of time.

He sat down at his desk and looked across at Wilkins. 'Have I missed anything exciting?'

Jack Wilkins looked up from his monitor. 'No, pretty quiet, though we have a post-mortem going on at the Royal Cornwall. I've put the report on your desk.'

Everett picked up the sheet keenly. He looked disappointed as he scanned it. 'A hobo found dead on the coastal path – it's not exactly a head-scratcher. Do we know him?'

Wilkins looked at his screen. 'The information has just come in. There was no ID on the body, but his fingerprints were in the system. His name is Duncan Fraser. He was forty-nine and grew up in Glasgow. Got a long history of mental illness and alcoholism, with a big list of charges ranging from violent affray to petty theft.'

'Next of kin?'

'No one. Only child, both parents deceased, never married.'

PC Sandra Kent felt moved to comment. 'How sad. Nobody would have been missing him when he went on the road and now nobody's giving a toss that he has been found dead.'

Everett was not so moved. 'Well, I wouldn't get too sentimental if I were you – by the sound of it he was a right charmless git.' He looked back at the report sheet. 'Any luck with the rucksack and banjo?'

Wilkins shook his head. 'Nothing turned up so far. We had a good look on the path itself. I'm sure they'll appear sooner or later.'

Everett was beginning to get interested once more. 'Curious they have gone missing, though. When do we get the PM results?'

'Doc Harrington reckons tomorrow morning. From the number of statements from people that Fraser encountered, it sounds like he has been sleeping rough on that stretch of the path for a month or so.'

Everett was thinking it through. 'The cigarette burns could have happened anytime, judging by the number of arguments he was provoking. Probably natural causes –

most likely he bedded down for the night and never woke up.'

'It doesn't explain the missing rucksack and banjo.'

Everett found himself nodding in agreement. 'Keep me informed. Now I must address my priorities. I'm off to get something to eat.'

With that he left the office with a bang of the door.

*

Daniel scratched the back of his head as he got up slowly from the bed. He looked at the time; it was five o'clock in the afternoon. He had been asleep for about two hours. By the time he had entered the cottage after the encounter with the policeman, he had felt shattered. Even after drinking his much-anticipated cup of tea, it had failed to revive him. He had lain on the bed struggling to rationalise all that had happened in the last twelve hours. In the end he had given up and surrendered to his fatigue. He went into the shower room and splashed his face with cold water. Feeling refreshed, he went downstairs, grabbed his coat and left the cottage. He wanted to talk to Luke.

Walking through the village, he noticed a narrow lane off to the left that seemed to rise steeply. He turned into it and hoped that once at the top, he could get a good signal on his phone. Nearing the summit, he noticed a strong smell of burning coming from beyond the hedge. He assumed it was probably an agricultural fire and thought no more of it. Finally reaching the top of the lane, he discovered it opened out onto a small churchyard with a small, attractive parish church. He walked a few steps into the graveyard that fronted the old stone structure and took in his surroundings. The silence and stillness made him feel extremely peaceful. He glanced at his phone. The signal looked strong. He rang Luke's number.

Luke answered promptly. 'Hello, Daniel, how's it going?'

'What would you say if I said a bit weird?'

'In what way?'

'Well, it would seem that not all of the natives are as friendly as the landlord in the Jolly Pirate for a start. There are some people that definitely do not want me here. Secondly, a body was found this morning on the coastal path just yards from the cottage.'

Luke was incredulous. 'What! Not murdered?'

'Don't think so, though it would not surprise me. I passed him on the path yesterday. He was a Scot. Let's just say he was not doing much for Anglo-Scottish relations.'

'And to think I sent you there for some peace and quiet.'

'The police interviewed me this afternoon, so I had to give your name as the owner of the Chough.'

Luke could not believe what he was hearing. 'Sounds like there is more going on down there than in London. Sure you're not exaggerating the hostility of the locals?'

Daniel remembered the damaged Fiat. 'Definitely not. Wait till you see the state of your car.'

'What, vandalised?'

'Let's just say someone's been busy with a key.'

Luke had heard enough. He made a decision. 'I'm coming down on Thursday afternoon – the sooner the better by the sound of it.'

'It would be nice to have a TV.'

'You sure? It sounds like you are getting more than enough entertainment.'

'It would be a welcome distraction.'

'Don't worry, I'll get it sorted. See you Thursday.'

Daniel was pleased that Luke had brought his visit forward. Apart from everything else, he could do with the company. Descending the hill his eyes settled on two young men about a hundred yards ahead of him. They were walking back down the lane towards the village. Judging by the raised voices, it sounded like they were having an argument. Daniel decided to hang back a little. There was something about their body language that urged caution. Then he recognised one of them. It was the hostile young fella from the Jolly Pirate.

*

Dennis Ashley was awoken out of his doze by the buzzer at the front door. As was usually his habit, he had fallen asleep in his chair in front of the telly. He looked at the clock on his mantel over the fireplace. The hands were showing half-past nine. He went to the intercom panel and could see that the light for Daniel Felton was flashing. *Not another one*, he thought. Throughout the day there had been several callers enquiring where they could reach Daniel. Since the cousin had visited that morning, he calculated it had been at least four. A couple of them had looked presentable enough, but by the look of the others he had his doubts. They were asking too many personal questions for his liking. One individual in particular had appeared almost immediately after Luke Sadler had left. After he had inadvertently let slip that the cousin had called, the man had seemed very insistent on getting his name. He had been very resolute in telling the unsavoury individual that he could not give out that information. He was looking forward to a repeat episode of *New Tricks* at ten, so he wanted to deal with the caller swiftly. He spoke into the intercom. 'Daniel is away at the moment. Don't know for sure when he's coming back.'

A deep, official-sounding voice replied, 'Is that, Mr Ashley, the landlord?'

'It is.'

'I am a representative of the Law Enforcement Agency. We need to speak with you on a very important matter.'

'Is it to do with Daniel?'

The voice sounded very authoritative. 'We cannot have this conversation over the intercom, Mr Ashley. It should not take too long.'

He hesitated for a few seconds before answering, 'I can give you ten minutes.'

'That's all we need, sir.'

A few minutes later, Dennis Ashley found himself faced with two large men in Daniel's room. Smartly dressed in suits, one of them flashed up some sort of ID card in front of his face. Suddenly he began to feel a little intimidated.

'Are you from the police?'

'Not exactly, sir, but our work does cross over from time to time.'

Ashley thought he detected a slight smirk play around the man's lips, only for it to vanish almost immediately.

The other man seemed to be taking no interest in the conversation, seeming to be more intent on snooping around Daniel's room behind his back. Ashley felt distinctly uncomfortable.

The man in front of him looked steadily into his eyes. 'Now, Mr Ashley, it is of the utmost importance that we find Daniel. We feel his life could be in danger.'

Ashley felt a slight dryness in his mouth as he spoke. 'I really cannot tell you where he is.'

'Could you think of anyone who might know?' His voice seemed to take on a deeper tone as he added, 'Think very carefully before you answer.'

The other man behind him had stopped snooping and was now also staring at Ashley. The expression on his face was strangely chilling, empty of all emotion.

Ashley slightly stuttered his reply. 'There… there is a cousin.'

The man pulled out a notebook. 'Now we are getting somewhere. Do you have a name?'

There was just the briefest of hesitation before Ashley answered, 'Luke Sadler.'

THREE
UNDER SUSPICION

Kate could not believe what she was hearing. 'Trouble seems to be following him about.'

Luke replied, 'I know, you couldn't make it up. I sent him down there for a quiet life.'

They were both curled up on the sofa in their Victoria Park house. A Michael Buble album played soothingly in the background. Luke was telling Kate of the telephone call with Daniel earlier in the day.

Kate tried to rationalise the information. 'I can understand the dead body, that's just bad luck, a case of being in the wrong place at the wrong time. It's the hostility from the locals that's worrying in view of your plans for next summer.'

Luke nodded. 'Exactly, that's why I have decided not to hang about and take a trip down there on Thursday.'

A thought occurred to Kate. 'You can't risk taking the Audi – we don't want that damaged.'

'Shit, I didn't think of that.'

'We can't spare another company car.'

Luke thought of his options. 'I can find a place to stay in Helston. Leave the car there and get a cab into Tregarris. Daniel can drive me back.'

Kate nodded. 'Sounds like a plan.'

'I've arranged for a TV delivery on Thursday afternoon. Poor sod sounds like he needs some relaxation. So far it's not gone as well as I'd planned; he wasn't supposed to get any stress. I hope he is not tempted to start gambling again… or do anything silly.'

Kate looked concerned. 'Do you think there's a chance that he would?'

Luke took her hand. 'Who knows, but I'm not taking any chances. I took a look through his mobile messages. He's got some problems. I'll take his phone with me so we can go through some of them.'

'I haven't told Lauren anything so far, but I can't stall her forever.'

Luke leaned over and gently kissed her forehead. 'I know, hun. Hopefully, by this time next week we'll have him in a better situation.'

'Just as a matter of interest, can I ask how much this is going to cost you?'

Luke gave her an earnest expression. 'Can you really put a price on the people you love?'

Kate cuddled up to him. 'I had a feeling you'd say something like that. It's probably why I love you.'

*

It was a quiet Wednesday morning in Helston Police

Station. Sergeant Jack Wilkins was making himself busy, sifting through some paperwork. Sandra Kent was sitting opposite, looking at her monitor. The unusually peaceful atmosphere in the station could be explained by the absence of DI Everett, who was out of the office giving evidence on a previous case at the law court in Truro.

Sandra looked across at Jack Wilkins. 'Is there anything back on the rough sleeper post-mortem, Sarge?'

Wilkins took a big swig of his coffee before answering. 'Nothing so far – the doc's report should be coming through anytime.'

'Did you get the feeling that there was anything suspicious when you saw the body?'

Wilkins thought back to the scene from the previous day. 'It looked a stonewall case of natural causes when I first arrived at the body site. But then when the information came out about the missing rucksack and banjo, it started to look more sinister. Of course, the doc put the seal on it with his discovery of the burn marks on the neck.'

'DI Everett will be a happy copper if the PM reveals it's not natural causes. You know how he appreciates a good mystery.'

'That he most certainly does. I know he can be a noisy, arrogant bugger, but you have to give him his due, his clear-up stats are very impressive.'

'I know. I just wish he wouldn't shout it from the rooftops.'

Wilkins laughed. 'I can't disagree with you on that one.'

They both appreciated these moments when they felt free to let off some steam regarding their superior.

Though Everett had excellent detecting qualities, there were times when working with him that you had to have the tolerance of a saint. Wilkin's email pinged. It was from the doc. There was an attachment containing his report.

It took only a few seconds of scrutiny before Wilkins announced, 'It definitely looks like we have a manslaughter on our hands.'

Sandra immediately rose from her desk and walked over to join him. As she read the report over his shoulder, she could not resist commenting, 'DI Everett's going to love this.'

*

Joe Blades was sitting at his desk in his Soho office. In front of him sat Private Investigator Mark Reid. He had instructed his two heavies, Vince and Max, to pay a visit to Daniel's landlord, in order to intimidate him just enough to get the name of the cousin. Blades decided that Mr Reid did not need to know anything about that.

'Luke Sadler is the name of the cousin. Hopefully he will be able to lead you to Daniel.'

Mark Reid wrote the name in his notebook. 'That should be all I need to work with.'

'Excellent. Let me know if you need anything else.'

Reid could guess that a certain amount of pressure must have been exerted on the landlord to get hold of the name. But he wasn't there to question beyond his remit of finding the whereabouts of Daniel. There were times when the job was much easier the less you knew. This was obviously one of them. He got up to leave. 'I will do some digging on this fella and report back.'

Joe Blades sat back in his chair looking satisfied. Mr Reid had asked no further questions and obviously knew the lines not to be crossed. 'Soon as you can, Mr Reid, soon as you can.'

*

It was mid-morning, and Daniel was lounging on the sofa in the cottage sipping a glass of lemonade. Though far from perfect, he had managed to grab a bit more sleep than the previous evening. Thankfully, there had been no repeat of the bell-ringing in the early hours. He had just returned from the convenience store, after stocking up on some household products and food provision. From what he had overheard in snatched conversations, some of the people in the village were still talking about the Scottish vagrant found dead from the day before. Thinking back to his encounter with the unfortunate Angus Fraser on the path, Daniel muttered to himself, 'Poor sod.' Looking at how easily his own desperate situation had rapidly developed, he did wonder what circumstances had triggered the downward spiral for the destitute Scot.

He eventually found his thoughts turning once again to Lauren. He realised now, that with the torment of his gambling urge reducing by the day, his affection for Lauren was coming more to the surface. What a twenty-four carat idiot he had been! Beginning to feel more despondent with every second, he rose from the sofa and went over to the window. Earlier that morning it had looked like rain was likely, but the threatening clouds had since lightened and the weather was dry. He decided to go for a walk.

*

Jack Wilkins and Sandra Kent sat silently as DI Everett scanned the post-mortem report on Duncan Fraser. He had returned from the court case in Truro in a good mood. The crucial evidence he had provided having secured a conviction for a particularly nasty piece of work. He looked up from the screen. 'According to the doc, a single kick to the chest could have administered the bruising to the upper cavity, vicious enough to rupture his spleen and bring on a cardiac arrest within the hour.'

Wilkins added, 'Seems like he could have been saved if he had been found earlier.'

Everett answered, 'Saved from what? Don't you think that his life was miserable enough? The doc says that he did not have long anyway. The attacker has probably done him a favour.'

'Maybe so, but we still owe it to him to find his killer.'

Everett banged a hand down on his desk. 'Of course we do, and we will.'

Sandra Kent picked up the original scene of crime report and handed it to Everett. Again there was a silence while he went over the report once again. After a few minutes he stood up. 'First we should get the posters out around Tregarris, informing about the rucksack and banjo. Also get it out to the local newspapers about the search for these items.'

Sandra answered, 'Yes, sir. I'll get in touch with the *Helston Advertiser* and the *Falmouth Packet*.'

'They will do for a start.'

Jack Wilkins pointed out, 'The crime scene officers did pick up some cigarette butts nearby; they now take on a new significance with regards to the cigarette burns on the neck.'

Everett nodded his agreement. 'The doc seemed quite positive that they were recent wounds.'

Sandra sounded outraged. 'Looks like it wasn't enough to kick the poor bastard; they thought they would throw in a little bit of torture as well.'

Everett turned on her. 'Now we don't know that for certain yet. It never pays to jump to conclusions.' He looked at Wilkins. 'Jack, think this guy in the cottage could have a hand in it?'

Wilkins thought back to his conversation with the young man at the Chough cottage. 'I don't see him as the attacker. Though I got the distinct impression that something was not quite right.'

Everett was interested. 'In what way exactly?'

'I got the impression he was not being totally straight.'

'You say he was staying in the cottage alone?'

'He said the cottage had been recently purchased by his cousin.'

Everett looked back at the report. 'A Luke Sadler. I think we should check him out.' He posed the obvious question. 'Why would a young man from London choose to stay in a remote cottage on his own at this time of the year?'

'My thoughts exactly.'

'Go along and interview him once again. Put him under some stronger interrogation, see how he reacts.' He looked across to Sandra Kent. 'I think it would be a good idea if you go along with Sergeant Wilkins to add a bit of pressure. See if you can spot any guilty body language.'

'Yes, sir.'

He looked back at the report. 'Don't you think it's interesting that Miss Thomson had seen his car outside the cottage earlier in the day? Where did he go? What was he doing?'

Wilkins replied, a little flippantly, 'Dumping the rucksack and banjo, perhaps?'

Everett allowed himself a grin and clapped his hands. 'You never know. Now let's get to it.'

*

Sergeant Wilkins rang the cast-iron bell for the second time. He and Sandra Kent were standing outside the Chough cottage. He peered into the front window. The cottage appeared to be empty. He looked across to Daniel's car parked outside. 'He surely can't still be in bed.'

Kent was looking up at the upstairs windows. 'He's probably gone out for a walk.'

'That's probably the answer.'

Sandra walked over to Daniel's car. It did not take her long to spot the deeply etched scratch along the side of the bodywork. 'It looks like some numb-brain has keyed his car.'

Wilkins sounded interested. 'Is that right?' He joined her beside the car and studied the damage. There was no doubt about it. In his career he had seen too much wanton vandalism not to recognise it when he saw it. They were still looking at the car when Daniel appeared, walking back from the direction of the coastal path.

*

Daniel was nearing the end of his walk. He had ambled a few miles along the path in the opposite direction from his previous excursion and had found the views equally as captivating. Once again he had felt his spirits rising with every step along the way. There was something about the sound of surf and gull that seemed able to generate a natural high. Turning inland towards the cottage, he was taken a little by surprise when he saw the two uniformed officers standing beside his car.

Sergeant Wilkins greeted him. 'Morning, Mr Felton. Been for a morning constitutional?'

Daniel answered genially, 'It definitely blows the cobwebs away.'

Wilkins pointed to the damage on Daniel's car. 'When did this happen?'

Daniel hesitated for a split second. In view of his situation, he thought the less attention and fuss he drew from the local police the better. The last thing he needed was the police investigating a petty crime on his behalf. 'I'm not exactly sure when I first noticed it. It's one of my cousin's company cars; it could have happened anywhere.'

'You don't think the vehicle could have sustained the damage since you arrived?'

'I doubt it, everyone seems so friendly here.'

Wilkins flashed Sandra Kent a glance before replying, 'Believe me, Mr Felton, like any other place, Cornwall has its share of bad apples.'

'I'm disappointed to hear it.' Daniel looked at their serious expressions. 'Is this visit to do with the dead Scotsman?'

Sandra Kent was looking at Daniel's face keenly as Wilkins answered, 'Yes, Mr Felton. We have identified him as Duncan Fraser. Unfortunately his death is not as straightforward as at first appeared.'

Daniel thought back to the Scot's belligerent manner. Somehow he was not surprised. 'Someone attacked him?'

'It looks like he took a heavy kick in the chest. That was all it took. He was in such bad physical condition.'

Both officers were studying Daniel's reaction to this information with keen attention.

'Poor man.'

Wilkins glanced over at the cottage. 'Would it be possible for us to take a peek inside the cottage, Mr Felton?'

Daniel was momentarily taken by surprise with this request. It then suddenly occurred to him that he was being seriously considered as a possible suspect. He showed them towards the doorway. 'Of course, no problem.'

*

Mark Reid took another bite of his panini as he looked at the doorway of Sadler's estate agents in Hoxton. He was sitting in his car which he had parked a little way along on the opposite side of the road. It had not taken him long to track down Luke Sadler. In fact, it had been ridiculously easy. His high profile on the internet as a very successful estate agent had ensured that. He stared admiringly at Sadler's black Audi A3 which was parked outside. He phoned in to Joe Blades' office. 'Hello, Mr Blades, this is Mark Reid.'

'Hello, Mr Reid, do you have anything to report?'

'I am sitting outside Luke Sadler's estate agent's office as we speak.'

Blades was intrigued. 'Go on.'

'It turns out that Mr Sadler is a bit of a whiz in the property business. In short, I think he is loaded.'

Blades struggled to keep the eagerness out of his voice. 'You don't say.'

'Not only does he own two offices in fashionable Hoxton, but from the looks of his internet profile, he is also building a pretty impressive property portfolio.'

This was music to Joe Blades' ears. It meant that there was more than a good chance of him getting his money back twofold. Who would have thought it? Daniel Felton had a rich cousin. More significantly, a rich cousin who, it appeared, was eager to help him. 'What's your next move?'

'Simple, I plan to follow him home tonight. His Audi is parked outside the office. It's a good chance that he will lead me to Daniel at some stage.'

Blades sounded much encouraged. 'Let me know as soon as you get something.'

'Will do.'

Blades put the phone down and fiddled distractedly

with his wrist bracelet. This was looking more promising than even he had first supposed.

*

'Where did you go on the Tuesday morning?' Jack Wilkins and Sandra Kent were sitting on the sofa in the Chough cottage drinking a cup of tea. Daniel stood in front of them feeling a little unsettled. Both officers had just returned to the lounge after completing a thorough search of the cottage.

'I spent the morning in Helston.'

'Can anyone vouch for you?'

Daniel thought for a second. 'Not really, though I did buy a couple of shirts in Coggleshall Street. They might remember me.' Kent wrote this down on her notepad.

Wilkins went on. 'You said you had an altercation with Duncan Fraser the day before?'

'Hardly an altercation – basically he just shouted abuse at me as we passed.'

'You didn't abuse him back?'

'No. It was obvious he was mentally unstable. I never took it personally. I won't deny that I did feel a bit intimidated... being alone with him on the path.'

'Which brings us to why you are down here from London, alone in Tregarris and out of the holiday season?'

Daniel realised that it probably did look a little odd and, in the present circumstances, maybe a touch suspicious.

'I have been going through a bit of a tough time recently... personal stuff.' Wilkins encouraged him to expand. 'I recently split with my girlfriend and quit my job. I was down in the dumps so my cousin thought it would be a good idea for me to get away for a bit. He had recently bought this cottage, so it seemed convenient.'

'Can you give me your cousin's telephone number?'

'Sure.'

Sandra Kent wrote the number as he read it from his phone.

Wilkins cut to the chase. 'Were you in the cottage on Monday evening?'

'No, I spent the evening in the pub, the Jolly Pirate on the high street.'

'About what time did you leave the pub?'

'It must have been sometime after eleven o'clock.'

Wilkins seized on a casual line of enquiry. 'Sounds like you had a good session, Mr Felton.'

Daniel felt himself answer maybe a bit too defensively. 'It was only about four pints.'

Both Wilkins and Kent picked up on his momentary anxiety. 'After leaving the pub, you didn't see anything or hear noises coming from the coastal path?'

Daniel thought back to the voice in the bush. Should he mention it? Was it relevant? He was suddenly feeling distinctly uncomfortable under the sergeant's intense gaze. It was a few seconds before he finally answered, 'No, apart from the sound of the surf it was very quiet.'

'You are quite sure, sir?'

'Definitely.'

The two officers rose from the sofa. Jack Wilkins spoke as he went to the door. 'That's all for now, Mr Felton, we will be in touch. Be sure to let us know if you see or think of anything that may throw some light on it.'

'I will, Officer.' Daniel closed the door and breathed deeply. He had found the police visit more than a little stressful.

*

Mark Reid kept his eyes fixed on the road ahead. The black Audi A3 was cruising three cars ahead of him. He had watched as Luke Sadler left his Hoxton Square office, accompanied by what appeared to be his girlfriend. The winter nightfall and early evening traffic was giving him good cover as he tracked Sadler's rear lights across East London. They had now turned off the Cambridge Heath Road into Victoria Park Road. He had the feeling that they were getting closer to their final destination. Sure enough, Sadler slowed down and turned into the residential area of Gore Street. Reid pulled over and parked the car. He watched the Audi travel a further hundred yards and stop in front of a row of fine-looking Victorian houses. Sadler and the girl got out of the car and mounted a short flight of steps before entering the house. After a couple of minutes, Reid left his car and strolled casually up to the house. Making a mental note of its location, he noticed that it directly overlooked the park on the opposite side of the street. Looking back towards the house, he wondered if Daniel Felton was also inside. He knew that only a combination of patient surveillance and stealthy tracking would give him the answer. He walked swiftly back to his car to give Mr Blades an update.

*

'So, what did you make of our solitary young man in the cottage?' DI Everett was addressing the question to Sandra Kent. It was early evening in Helston HQ and they were discussing the suspected manslaughter case of Duncan Fraser.

Kent answered thoughtfully, 'Well, his explanation for why he is staying in the cottage seems plausible enough.'

Jack Wilkins agreed. 'I suppose it makes sense. If you believe everything he said to be true, then it looks like he is in the middle of some sort of personal crisis. He's given me his cousin's phone number, so I can check out his story.'

Everett was scanning Sandra's written report of their visit to the cottage. 'Did the clothes shop in Coggleshall Street confirm he was in Helston on the morning the body was found?'

Sandra replied, 'Yes, the girl in the shop remembered him in particular because of his good looks.'

Everett was unimpressed. 'There are any number of places he could have dumped the rucksack and banjo on his way into Helston. You found nothing suspicious or incriminating in the cottage?'

Wilkins answered, 'Nothing to put him in the frame. In fact, the place was all a bit on the sparse side. Looks like it still needs a bit of work doing.'

Everett was reading over the report once more. 'So on the Monday evening he came back to the cottage after the pub closed… probably drowning his sorrows. Still, begs the question. He had already had an altercation with Fraser earlier in the day. Who's not to say that with a few beers inside him, he bumped into Fraser on the way back to the cottage and got provoked into chasing him onto the path and giving him a kick?'

Kent recalled the damage to Daniel's car. She looked across to Jack Wilkins. 'Is it possible he might have caught Fraser vandalising his car and lost his temper?'

Wilkins thought back to the mild-mannered Londoner and his rather vague answers regarding the car damage. He found it hard to imagine, but four pints of beer can change some people, especially someone who is going through a bad time personally.

Everett was warming to the theory. 'Finding your car being keyed by the same man who had already abused you earlier in the day is pretty provocative, especially after sinking a few pints. Don't you think?'

Sandra Kent remarked, 'He was definitely a bit twitchy under questioning.'

Wilkins agreed, 'He gave the impression that he was holding something back.'

Everett thought of the cigarette burns on Fraser's neck. 'Any sign that he is a smoker?'

Sandra thought back to Daniel's clean-cut looks and white teeth. 'I doubt it, certainly not from what we could see in the cottage.'

Wilkins nodded. 'Of course, he could be a social puffer, someone who likes an occasional fag with a beer.'

Kent thought that suspecting Daniel as a sadist was a step too far. 'I just don't see Mr Felton as a torturer.'

Everett was quick to advise her. 'Believe me, Sandra, in my time I have seen some of the most evil deeds perpetrated by what appeared to be the most angelic of people.' He turned to Jack Wilkins. 'Well, first thing to do is check out his story with the cousin.'

Wilkins went over to his desk. 'I'll get on to it right away.'

*

Luke Sadler was lying stretched out on his sofa in front of the television. He was watching a documentary about luxury hotels around the world, but he was finding it hard to concentrate. His plan was to drive straight on to Cornwall in the morning, after first dropping off Kate at the office in Hoxton. He had booked a room for the night in the Strathallan Guest House in Helston. He did not think he would need the bed, but the important thing was that it provided safe parking. In view of what Daniel had told him about the company Fiat, he did not want to take any chances with the Audi. Upstairs, he could faintly hear Kate singing along to Taylor Swift in the bath. He did not like leaving her alone in the week, even for one night, but he felt the situation with Daniel and the cottage had left him no choice. Besides which, he was going with Kate's full backing. It was in both their interests – plus Lauren's – to get Daniel sorted. Also, purely from a self-interested point of view, he needed to quickly sort out the local hostility issue. He tried to get his attention back on the TV but then his mobile rang. He did not recognise the number.

'Hello.'

'Good evening. This is Sergeant Wilkins from the Devon and Cornwall County Police.'

Luke had suspected that he might get a call from the police after his last conversation with Daniel.

The sergeant went on. 'Am I talking to Mr Luke Sadler?'

'Yes.'

'Sorry for interrupting your evening, Mr Sadler, but I would appreciate if you could confirm a few details relating to your cousin Daniel Felton.'

'Sure, no problem.'

'It's just routine enquiries, you understand. He says he is staying in your cottage in Tregarris. Is that correct?'

'Yes, that is certainly correct, Officer.'

'From what he has told us, it seems that on a personal level he has been going through a tough time recently.'

Luke was not sure how much detail Daniel had given, but the sergeant obviously wanted some sort of confirmation. 'That's true, Officer, he has hit a bit of a crossroads in his personal life. I thought it would be a good time for him to get away from London for a bit.'

'Have you had any contact with Daniel since he left London?'

'He phoned me yesterday. He told me about the unfortunate man who was found dead on the coastal path.' The pause at the other end of the line made Luke feel uneasy. 'Daniel is not in any trouble, is he?'

There was a further pause before the sergeant replied, 'Well, the post-mortem has since confirmed that the death was not down to natural causes, so we have to conduct a thorough investigation. With Daniel being in the cottage so near to the body site, he obviously comes under scrutiny.'

Luke could hardly believe what he was hearing. He thought it typical that only Daniel could find himself in this situation. 'I can assure you, Officer, that Daniel is one of the most passive people I know.'

'He certainly comes across as a decent sort, Mr Sadler, but we obviously have to do our job.'

'I understand that, Officer. As it happens I am coming down to see him tomorrow.'

'Well then, I hope you have a good journey, Mr Sadler. Much appreciate your cooperation.' Having sensed Sadler's seemingly genuine concern for his cousin, he added, 'You have my number if you need it.'

In view of the way things seemed to be panning out for Daniel, Luke thought that the number might well prove useful. 'No problem. Thanks.'

Luke shook his head as he rang off. He turned off the TV and made his way upstairs. Halfway up the steps he shouted, 'Kate, wait till you hear the latest.'

On the street outside Luke Sadler's house, Mark Reid drummed his fingers restlessly on the steering wheel. In the hope of catching a glimpse of Daniel Felton, he had now been waiting there for the best part of four hours. Disappointingly, there had been no sign of him so far. He reasoned to himself that there was still a good chance that Felton was in the house, but years of experience and finely-honed intuition told him differently. If his instincts proved to be correct then at some point he would have to fix a GPS tracking device on Sadler's car. Acutely aware of his growing hunger, he decided there was no point in waiting around any longer. He started the engine of his Ford Fiesta. He planned to return in the early morning.

*

Daniel was having another restless night. He had been sleeping on and off, but now he felt wide awake. His mind felt like it was in overdrive. He looked at the time on his mobile; it was coming up to three o'clock. He turned over in the bed for the umpteenth time... and then he heard it. The cast-iron bell at the door rang loud and clear. For a split second he froze, before rising from the bed and going to the window. Straining to see in the gloom, it appeared that as before, there was nobody to be seen. As he stared down at the partly obscured doorway, the bell rang loudly once more. He stood transfixed at the window for the next few minutes, expecting at any moment to see a shadowy figure emerge in the darkness. But no such figure appeared. As he watched, a gentle coastal mist appeared to float towards the doorway. It began to form into swirling, twisting shapes. The effect was almost hypnotic; and then he saw it. It had been fleeting but he had definitely seen it. For the briefest of moments, the mist had somehow evolved itself into a hazy human silhouette. He felt a cold shiver go down his spine. He moved away from the window. For one panic-stricken moment, he seriously felt like he was going mad. He made a determined effort to regain his composure and told himself that the vision could only have been a product of his fevered imagination. But it was still no explanation for the bell ringing at the door. That was very real. Feeling unnerved and very alone, he sat down on the bed and put his head into his trembling hands. In that moment he felt desperately close to tears.

*

In the bedroom of an old tin miner's house, just a few miles away from the Chough cottage, a young man reached under his bed to grab an old muslin sack, much soiled by mud and grime. As he pulled it towards him, the sack emitted the faint sound of metal string on hollowed wood. He reached in and pulled out a musical instrument. He laughed softly to himself as his fingers began to strum it gently.

FOUR

NO HIDING PLACE

M ark Reid's Ford Fiesta turned slowly into Gore Road and pulled into the kerb. After returning home for something to eat and managing to grab a few hours' sleep, he was back in the street watching Luke Sadler's house. As he had hopefully anticipated, the road was dark and quiet, with no lights showing in any of the house windows. The digital clock in the car told him it was four o'clock in the morning. He did not have too long before the early risers would start getting up for work. He reached for an object on the passenger seat and went to open the car door. A movement out of the corner of his eye caused him to freeze. A figure was approaching on the opposite side of the road. He leant sideways and kept low in the car, as the footsteps drew closer before passing by on the other side of the street. The early morning commuter was a further reminder that he had no time to waste. He opened his car door and approached Sadler's Audi swiftly from behind. Crouching down, he then carefully placed the GPS tracking device inside the rear wheel arch on the driver's side. He was back in his own car within seconds.

*

Luke Sadler finished his last mouthful of cornflakes, before shouting up to the bathroom. 'Hurry up, Kate, I want to be on the road in five minutes.' He could just about hear a muffled reply of acknowledgement coming from upstairs. He went through his checklist: Daniel's iPhone, new supply of pants and socks, cash and change of clothing. He was ready to go.

Kate appeared in the kitchen looking slightly harassed. 'We're running earlier than I expected; I will have to have the spare keys for the office.'

Luke handed her the keys. 'I don't know why you take so much time getting ready. You look lovely as you are.'

Kate scoffed and gave him a push. 'I like to think we have moved on from the stage where you feel you still have to give me that old hogwash.'

Luke laughed as he protested his innocence. 'I'm being serious. Look… I have my sincere face on.'

It was Kate's turn to laugh. 'I think it needs more practice.'

Luke adopted a pained expression. 'Ouch! That hurts.' He changed the subject. 'We ready to go?'

Kate slipped on her coat and picked up her bag. She smiled. 'You drive carefully on the way down. I don't want anything happening to the Audi.'

Luke pulled a face. 'Charming!' He turned towards the door. 'Right, now let's get Daniel sorted.'

'Hope it goes well. I'm seeing Lauren for lunch. It would be nice to be able to tell her something positive.'

'Let's hope so.' As an afterthought Luke added, 'It might be a good idea to invite Lauren to stay over tonight. Give you a good chance to chat.'

'You must have read my mind.'

Luke smiled. 'You know what they say, great minds and all that.' Luke picked up his bag and they left the house together.

*

Daniel sat distractedly on the sofa. He had overslept after the disturbing events of the early morning. He had been trying to rationalise what he had seen, before finally putting it all down to stress. The police visit had been unsettling. Though he was innocent, he realised that he had made a bit of a mess of convincing the investigating officers. He drained his teacup and stood up to stretch. He was glad that Luke was coming down to see him. He felt he needed to talk – not only about his situation – but also to keep his sanity: and then of course there was Lauren. He opened the front door and gazed at the cast-iron bell with the tattered strap. Seeing it swaying gently in the breeze, it seemed a lot less menacing in the daylight. Somehow it looked at odds with the rest of the cottage… too old, too ancient. More inexplicably, whose hand had been ringing it in the early hours?

*

'He looks like he's heading towards the South West.' Mark Reid was looking at the GPS tracker as he spoke to Joe Blades on his car phone. 'He dropped his girlfriend off at the Hoxton office first thing this morning and then headed across London to the M4. I followed him as far as Chiswick before turning back.'

Blades sounded disappointed. 'It might explain Felton's disappearing act. Sadler has probably got him tucked away somewhere down there.'

Reid was still studying the GPS. 'It looks like he's just stopped at a motorway service centre on the M5 near Exeter.'

'OK, keep me posted where he ends up. Where are you at the moment?'

'I am parked outside his estate agents. I can see his girlfriend through the window.'

'Just might pay to keep your eye on her movements as well.'

'That is my intention.'

'Speak to you later.'

Blades leant back in the chair and smoothed his hair. It looked like the search for Felton was going to take a little more time.

Mark Reid was just beginning to think about his lunch when the door of the estate agents opened and Sadler's girlfriend came out. He adjusted his rear mirror to get a better look. It looked like she was on the move. He watched as she got into a blue Fiat 500. He would have to put his lunch on hold. He started his car as she drove past.

*

Martin Everett gave a slight sigh of disappointment as he sat in front of his screen. He was studying the DNA report on the cigarette stubs found near the body of Duncan Fraser.

Jack Wilkins looked up. 'Anything wrong, sir?'

'The findings on the cigarette DNA test have just come in. Unfortunately there doesn't appear to be a match on the database.'

'That's a shame.'

Everett continued looking at his screen. 'It looks like it's going to take a little more digging to solve this one. Did you say that PC Kent is making enquiries in Tregarris this morning?'

'That's right, sir. As you would expect, there seems to be plenty of people in the village willing to talk about the incident. I think they find it all a little exciting.'

'That's the trouble. Everyone in the village will be eager to give their own theory. It will be a full-time job sorting out anything useful in the information.'

Wilkins offered a positive note. 'You would think that in a tight-knit community like Tregarris, there is more than a good chance that somebody will eventually spill the beans.'

'Let's hope so.'

*

A few miles south of Helston, on the high street of Tregarris, Sandra Kent was busily taking down statements from anyone who felt they could help in the enquiries. Unfortunately, much of what she was hearing was mainly based on conjecture and guesswork. On several occasions she had found herself tearing a page out of her notebook after reading it back and deciding it was worthless. Despite this lack of useful info, she was enjoying herself. It reminded her that engaging with the communities and talking to people was the part of the job that she found most satisfying.

She realised she had reached the end of the high street and turned back to look down its length. Tregarris was a typical Cornish village that until recently had been left behind in the booming tourist industry. In truth it was more of a hamlet than a village, with only the fine Norman church on the hill and the Jolly Pirate pub to recommend it. Until the recent fashion for holiday homes in secluded Cornish surroundings, the village had originally drawn most of its visitors by virtue of it being situated near the coastal path; but the recent increased demand for holiday homes signalled that was changing.

She turned back towards the path and walked past the Chough cottage. Daniel Felton's car was parked outside. She thought back to her first impressions of the mild-mannered Londoner. Could he really be capable of kicking a man to death? Despite DI Everett's suspicions, she found it hard to imagine. At the same time she could not deny that there was a nervousness about him that did not feel convincing.

She walked on to the coastal path and gazed out on the panorama. The slate-grey sky held a tint of blue on the horizon, as it merged into the sea. She drank in the view and inhaled the sea air. It was moments like this that made her glad she had accepted the transfer from Salisbury Central. Her thoughts went back to Daniel Felton and his stated reasons for being here. It was certainly true that there were times in life when you needed to get away and have a chance to reset. Had she not done the very same thing a year ago? At that time, upping sticks and leaving behind a failed relationship seemed the only solution left to her. Lost in her thoughts, she turned and retraced her steps back up the high street.

*

The minicab turned into the narrow road that led down to Tregarris. Luke Sadler sat forward in his seat as the village came into view. He had wasted little time in booking the cab after checking into the Strathallan Guest House in Helston. 'Straight to the end of the high street, driver, that will be fine.'

The driver could not resist a comment. 'They have had a bit of drama here in the last couple of days – man found murdered on the coastal path.'

Luke did his best to sound surprised. 'Really? I bet that has got the village buzzing.'

'They think the murderer must be a local.' The driver turned and grinned at Sadler. 'So you go careful.'

Sadler smiled back. 'I'll be sure to take your advice.'

The minicab pulled up in front of the cottage. The driver pointed towards the coastal path. 'It was just over there they found him – a Scottish drifter, so they say.'

Luke continued to act as if he was hearing of the murder for the first time. 'Really? Poor fella.' He paid the fare and got out of the cab. The driver waved from his open window. 'Thanks, remember to take care.'

As the cab drove off, Luke turned and noticed the damage to the company car's bodywork, which was parked outside the cottage. Whoever it was had done a good job. Why? The humble Fiat 500 was hardly a natural target for envious vandals. Shaking his head, he walked towards the front door of the Chough.

*

'The GPS is telling me that he arrived outside the Strathallan Guest House in Helston.' Once again Mark Reid was reporting in to Joe Blades from his car.

'Do you think that's where he has Felton tucked away?'

'There's a good chance, I would have thought.'

'So what's your next move?'

'Sadler could have gone down there to fetch him back. It's probably best to wait and see if that proves to be the case.'

'Where are you now?'

'I'm still outside the estate agents in Hoxton. I've just got back after Sadler's girlfriend took me on a little jaunt into the West End when she went for lunch.'

'Where did she go?'

'Selfridges in Oxford Street. Turned out she was meeting a girlfriend.'

'Keep me posted.' Joe Blades looked solemn as he ended the call. He would let Mr Reid carry on his work in leading him to Felton. Then it would be a job for Vince and Max.

Meanwhile Mark Reid reflected on his options. It seemed more than likely that Sadler's sudden visit to the West Country had something to do with his missing cousin. Having already spent some time hanging around the house in Victoria Park, he found it hard to imagine Daniel Felton lying low inside. He decided to return home and wait for the GPS to signal Sadler's return journey. He felt that there was a good chance that Felton might be returning with him. He started his car. It looked like a good opportunity to pick up a takeaway on the way home and put his feet up for a few hours.

*

'Luke, you are a diamond.' Daniel Felton was sitting in front of the fifty-inch Samsung TV that had just been delivered by the local Argos store in Helston.

Luke Sadler was standing behind him. 'I thought you would be pleased.'

When he had arrived earlier that morning, he had been more than a little concerned by the shabby appearance of his cousin. Daniel had explained it by immediately telling him of his disturbed night and the resultant lack of sleep. After Luke had informed him of Sergeant Wilkins's phone call, they had gone on to talk at some length about the issue of the car damage and the discovery of Duncan Fraser's body. Finally ordering his cousin to get shaved and take a shower, Luke had made himself busy in the kitchen area by conjuring up some bacon sandwiches. Now looking at Daniel's revived spirits and appearance, it was obvious that the treatment had worked. The delivery of the TV had been the icing on the cake. Luke knew that there would have to be some serious talking at some point, but seeing his cousin looking so much happier, he decided to bide his time and let Daniel enjoy the moment.

*

'So, to sum up, there was not a lot of useful info coming from the locals?' DI Everett was talking to Sandra Kent after she had recently returned from Tregarris.

She answered, 'Plenty of theories, but none of them seemed worthy of serious investigation. There is certainly no shortage of amateur sleuths in Tregarris.'

Everett was still interested. 'Would you care to run some of them past me?'

She gave a cynical chuckle. 'Anything from a bunch of Glasgow gangsters catching up with Fraser, to the countless people he upset on his travels that might be carrying a grudge. Unfortunately his aggressive manner tended to make enemies very easily.'

Jack Wilkins, who was sitting at his desk listening, thought back to the bystanders' comments on the day they found Fraser's body. He could not recall any that were remotely complimentary. 'He would not have won any popularity contest, that's for sure.'

Everett asked, 'Anything interesting relating to Daniel Felton?'

Sandra Kent frowned. 'There were a few people casting suspicion, mainly because of the fact that he was seen leaving the pub on his own that evening.'

Everett looked disappointed. 'Is that all?'

'Pretty much. Otherwise all the speculation seemed based on nothing more than the close proximity of the body to the Chough cottage and the fact that Felton's recent arrival coincided with Fraser's death.'

Everett thought of the cigarette butts. 'All the same, I think that purely for elimination purposes we should get a sample of Felton's DNA.'

Wilkins answered, 'We will get that sorted, sir.'

'Excellent. I'm sure we will soon get to the bottom of it.' Everett got up and looked at his watch. 'Right, I'm off for a bite to eat.' As was his usual custom, he left the office with a loud slam of the door.

Sandra Kent looked across at Jack Wilkins. 'I get the feeling he still thinks that Felton is the number-one suspect.'

Wilkins nodded slowly. 'Well, as it stands he is the only suspect.'

'What do you think, Sarge?'

'I think it's too early to say.' He could tell from her concerned expression that she hoped that Felton was not involved. He grinned. 'Am I detecting a certain soft spot for Mr Felton?'

For one brief moment he thought she looked a touch embarrassed. 'No, I just think he seems too decent a character to kick a man to death, let alone put lighted cigarettes on someone's neck.'

Wilkins looked at her earnest expression. Not for the first time he found himself drawn to her. Though not obviously pretty, she was not unattractive. In his more fanciful moments he would imagine asking her out, but the ten-year age difference and his general lack of confidence in the lady department held him back. Now in his mid-thirties, he was beginning to accept his single status as a permanent condition. In truth he had always felt awkward around girls, but somehow he felt different with Sandra. He felt relaxed in her company and they got on well. He found himself agreeing with her. 'I know what you are saying, but you can't deny his obvious uneasiness in the interview. Hopefully the DNA test will go some way to put him in the clear. We'll pay him a visit sometime in the morning.'

*

Luke Sadler tapped into the SMS inbox on Daniel's iPhone. There were about twenty voicemails and thirty messages. He was sitting alongside Daniel on the sofa. His cousin was engrossed in surfing through the channels on the new TV. 'Right, down to business, Daniel, I want you to tell me who is friend or foe.'

Daniel reluctantly put down the TV remote. 'That shouldn't take long. I don't think I have any friends left.'

They proceeded to scroll through the messages. There weren't many that were not requesting he paid back the money he owed. Apart from a few from Lauren and a couple of casual enquiries as to his welfare from old friends, it made grim reading. After painstakingly going through the texts with Daniel, Luke was left with a list of names and organisations that his cousin confirmed were respectable claims. It was Luke's intention to pay back every one of them. 'Now, you mentioned being threatened by two heavies.'

Daniel thought back to how he had felt that day when the two men had turned up at his bedsit. He had never felt so intimidated. 'They said they were collecting for someone and he would not be pleased if I didn't cough up. I'm sure the sum they were asking for was way off the mark.'

'Can you think of anyone it might be?'

Daniel thought back to the man who had approached him in the pub. 'There was a guy who got talking to me in my local, I'm pretty sure it must be him.'

'He offered you money?'

'Yes. Not straight away. He softened me up with some football talk at first. Looking back I was obviously targeted.'

Luke nodded. 'I don't think there's much doubt about that. Can you remember how much he gave you?'

'He arranged for someone to meet me outside the pub the next day. It was about two grand in an envelope.'

Luke could not believe what he was hearing. He had a desperate urge to tell his cousin what an idiot he had been, but he realised in that moment, it would not have been particularly helpful. Biting his lip, he asked, 'I am assuming that there was no credit agreement or paperwork involved in this transaction.'

'No, it was all very informal. It suited me at the time so I never questioned it.'

'How much did the two men demand?'

Daniel answered with a heavy sigh. 'Around six grand.'

Luke whistled softly. 'Please tell me you did not give them any personal documents?'

'They did ask for my passport for security, but I told them it was at my parents' house.'

Luke could not help letting out an exasperated sigh. 'Well, at least you had some sense left in that head of yours. How have you let yourself get in such a mess?'

'That's the frightening thing, Luke. I just don't know.'

Luke thought it was not much of an answer, but he had read somewhere: that was often the case with addiction. 'Well, I can tell you now, Daniel these men are not getting a penny. This dude the two men are working for is obviously a loan shark.'

Daniel looked apologetic. 'I'm truly sorry, Luke. I swear I'll never let you down again.'

Luke grinned to relieve the tension. 'Can you put that in writing?'

Daniel visibly relaxed and picked up the TV remote once more. 'Don't suppose you have heard anything from Lauren?'

'Are you starting to miss her?'

'What do you think? Being alone for a while with your thoughts, you start to realise what's important.'

'That was the idea of you coming down here. It's also good news that you haven't felt the urge to start gambling again.'

'I haven't given it a thought to be honest. It feels like my life back in London existed on another planet.'

'That's good to hear. As it happens, I think Lauren is staying at our place tonight.'

Daniel looked anxious. 'You haven't told her anything?'

'Not yet, though if it's your plan to try to get back with her she'll have to know at some time.'

Daniel knew his cousin was right. 'I'll tell her everything, I promise.'

Luke had an idea. 'Do you want us to bring her down here so you can tell her face to face?'

Daniel was silent for a few seconds before finally answering, 'Let me think about it.'

'Of course, it's your shout.' Luke got up from the sofa. 'Now, let's get that kettle on.'

*

It was early evening and Mark Reid was sat in front of his television. Every now and then he glanced at the GPS tracker: there was still no sign of movement. He had originally hoped that Sadler had driven down to Cornwall in order to pick up his cousin and bring him back that day. But now with the time fast approaching seven o'clock, that was beginning to seem increasingly unlikely. It looked like it was going to be another night in alone with his thoughts. He did not mind; he was getting used to it. Since his divorce, takeaway meals and lonely nights had become his new normal. Michael Portillo was on the TV, enthusing about one of his Great Rail journeys. Reid thought that perhaps he should try it sometime. The idea of just getting on a train and ending the journey in a strange location seemed attractive. Anything seemed better than his present existence. Had he begun to feel that way after he had left the police force? Or was it after the divorce? It was difficult to know for sure. Either way he knew he had felt unhappy for some time. The PI work could be a distraction, and could on occasion give him moderate satisfaction, but most of the time it was sordid work and left him feeling grubby. He got up and went to the kitchen. He fancied another cheese sandwich.

*

The evening atmosphere in the Jolly Pirate pub was building nicely. The village was still abuzz with the murder of Duncan Fraser, and as a consequence there was much conversation in the pub on the subject. Luke and Daniel had savoured a delicious scampi and chips meal in the restaurant area and had now got themselves seated in the public bar. Anyone seeing them seated together in the pub would probably have hazarded a guess that they were related. Same build with only a slight difference in colouring, they shared the same clean-cut good looks. It was only in the body language that you could see a marked difference. Daniel appeared slightly restless and unsure, whilst Luke appeared contained and steady, giving an impression of calm assurance. In spite of the occasional inquisitive glance from some of the locals, they were already well into their second pint of Tribute and beginning to enjoy themselves.

They were discussing the unexplained mystery of the ringing bell. After originally hearing Daniel's story, Luke had wasted little time in examining the bell to see if it was possible that the wind could have blown it. He had pushed and pulled the tattered strap in all directions but had soon dismissed that possibility. The cast-iron bell was far too heavy. It left him feeling pretty sure that those responsible for the damage to the Fiat had got something to do with it.

Daniel was not so certain. 'But every time I've looked out of the window, there's been no one there.'

'But you did say the view was not entirely clear.'

Daniel had no intention of risking ridicule by revealing what he thought he did see the last time he went to the window. 'Not entirely, but I would have thought clear enough if anyone was there.'

Luke thought of a logical answer. 'Perhaps it's some kind of trick. Whoever it was may have tied something to it and rang it from a distance.'

Daniel had to admit that could have been a possibility. 'I suppose so.'

'Did you say that it rang at the same time on both nights?'

'Yes, about three o'clock in the morning.'

A sudden thought flashed into Luke's mind. 'Isn't that the time on the broken grandfather clock?'

Daniel looked disturbed. 'Now you really are spooking me.'

Luke laughed. 'What a great story.'

'I'm glad you think so.'

'Well, if it rings tonight, I will be downstairs in a flash. Don't worry, we'll soon find out who the joker is.' Luke took a swill of his beer and looked appreciably around the pub. He nodded towards the landlord. 'The landlord seems a good fella.'

Daniel nodded. 'Yes, Reg seems a decent sort.' He looked across at the crowd of young men at the end of the bar. The tall, fair-haired youth was there again, still occasionally giving them a belligerent stare. Just what was his problem? He remarked to Luke, 'Unfortunately not all of the natives seem to be so amicable.'

Luke answered without looking across to the bar area. 'Yes, I had picked up on some hostile vibes.' He finished off his pint and stood up. 'Let's get another one in.'

Reg smiled genially as he served Luke another two pints of Tribute. 'Would I be right in thinking that you are the cousin that's purchased the Chough?'

'That's me.'

'Staying for long?'

'I'm going back to London tomorrow, but I'll probably be back sometime over the next week. My cousin will be sticking around for a little longer.'

'It's certainly exciting times around these parts at present.'

Luke guessed he was talking about the body found on the coastal path. 'Yes, I should imagine it's not every day you get a murder on your doorstep.'

'That's a fact – can't think of any in my time.' Reg changed the subject. 'Old Tom will be pleased that the Chough is in good hands.'

Luke was familiar with the name of the previous owner of the cottage. 'I like to think so. I've heard that old Tom was a good character?'

'He was one of my best customers, along with those two reprobates over there.' He pointed to the two old men sitting in the corner. They looked across and raised their glasses.

Luke raised his glass in turn. 'Cheers.' He thought it was a good opportunity for some public relations. 'Fill up their glasses, Reg, and have one yourself while you're at it.'

The landlord beamed. 'Don't mind if I do, sir. Cheers.'

Daniel had witnessed his cousin's generosity from where he was sitting. 'Cultivating the locals already,' he remarked, as Luke re-joined him.

'Always pays to get people on your side. I do eventually want to be able to park my car safely in the village, after all.'

'Good point.' Daniel pointed across to the two old men. 'Do you notice that they have a full pint in front of an empty chair? It was the same the other evening.'

Remembering the conversation with the landlord, Luke thought he knew the answer. 'I reckon that pint's meant for old, Tom. Reg told me he was a regular; those two were his mates.'

After Reg had served the two old men their pints, they raised their glasses in gratitude before beckoning for the two cousins to join them. Taking their chairs, the two cousins walked over and sat down with the old men at the table.

One of the men raised his glass. 'Yecki-da. My name's Alf, this is Billy.'

Luke tried to imagine their features through the mass of grey beard and ruddy complexions. 'My pleasure, I'm Luke and this is my cousin Daniel.' Luke raised his glass. 'Cheers.'

Alf suddenly leaned forward with interest. 'So how are you getting on in old Tom's cottage?'

Luke glanced across at Daniel before answering, 'It's been interesting so far to say the least.'

Billy pointed to the empty chair. 'That's where Tom used to sit with us every night.'

Luke tried out his theory. 'I'm guessing that this spare pint is meant for him.'

Alf nodded. 'It's been there waiting for him ever since he left us. Makes us feel like he is still here.'

Thinking about his recent unnerving experiences, Daniel was interested to know a bit more about the history of the Chough. 'How old is the cottage?'

Alf was keen to educate him. 'It goes back about three hundred years.' His eyes suddenly narrowed. 'It was an old pirate's house. He went by the name of Red Robbo.'

Luke took another swill of his beer. He was enjoying this conversation.

It was Billy's turn to lean forward. 'Have you wondered about the bell?'

Daniel gave a slight start. 'Well, it doesn't seem to quite fit in with the cottage. Why do you ask?'

Billy could not wait to reply. 'They say the bell used to belong to Red Robbo's ship, the *Black Dragon*.'

Daniel's mind went back to the misty images he had seen the night before. Once more he felt that familiar icy chill. 'Really?'

Billy went on, 'I can tell you something else. On the night that old Tom died...' Before he could say anything else, Billy gave a slight jump and rubbed his shin. Alf was staring at him sternly. It was obvious that Billy had been stopped in his tracks. There was an awkward silence before Luke changed the atmosphere by telling Daniel to get another round in.

Still wondering what Billy had been about to say, Daniel waited to be served at the bar. At that moment there appeared to be no one around to give attendance. Sitting on a bar stall in his usual position he recognised

Sid. He gave Daniel a friendly wink. 'Alright, my ansum? Reg has just gone down to change the barrel.'

'Thanks. My offer of a drink still stands, by the way.'

Sid looked at his near-empty glass. 'I don't deny, I am chacking.'

'You're more than welcome.'

Sid held his glass out. 'Go on then.'

Daniel became aware of someone standing behind him. Without having to fully turn around, he could just make out that it was the unfriendly fair-haired youth. Reg returned to the bar from downstairs and asked, 'Who's first?'

As Daniel went to order he heard a loud voice behind him say, 'Four pints of Proper Job, Reg.'

The publican glanced briefly at Daniel. He suspected that the young man from London should have been served first, but knowing Ricky Carlyon as he did, he decided to avoid the potential for aggravation. He proceeded to pull the pints. Daniel breathed deeply. This guy had been trying to provoke him ever since he had arrived. He refused to rise to the bait. After Carlyon retreated from the bar with his drinks, Sid, who had witnessed the provocative behaviour first-hand, gave Daniel a sympathetic smile. 'Don't mind Ricky, sometimes he can be as teezy as 'n adder.'

Daniel guessed that must be a Cornish phrase for bad attitude. He gave Sid a dismissive wave of the hand. 'No worries, the fella has obviously got a problem.' He bought Sid his pint and went back to the table with a tray of foaming pints.

Meanwhile back at the bar, Sid turned to Reg and shook his head. 'You're going to have to tell him sometime.'

Luke and Daniel finally rolled out of the Jolly Pirate just after closing time. Six pints of Tribute had put them in a carefree mood as they made their way back to the cottage. There was a slight slur in Luke's speech as he patted Daniel on the back. 'That was one great evening: authentic Cornishmen, talk of pirates, great beer, perfect.'

Daniel was not quite so enthused, but the beer had certainly relaxed him. 'What was that stuff about the bell? Billy was going to say something else before the other one stopped him.'

Luke laughed at the memory. 'Yeah! It was not exactly subtle. Let's say we take a quick peek at the sea before we turn in.' The two of them walked on past the cottage and headed for the coastal path.

They were not to know that in the darkness behind them, a figure stepped furtively out of the undergrowth and watched them go.

The two cousins stood taking in the view that lay before them. The sea looked like a shimmering millpond, with the low Autumn Hunter's moon illuminating the horizon. They could just about hear the water gently lapping on the rocks below. Luke took a look along the path. 'I suppose it was somewhere around here that they found the body.'

Daniel pointed to an area a few feet along the path. 'Around about there, I think.'

Luke looked back in the direction of the Chough cottage. It was quite close. He could see why a young stranger in the village like Daniel would come under police scrutiny.

Whether it was the effects of the beer or the picturesque view in front of him, Daniel suddenly sounded a little emotional. 'I can't thank you enough, Luke. It terrifies me to think what I would have done without you.'

Luke looked sideways at his cousin. In that moment he thought that Daniel looked almost childlike: frightened, lost and confused. He put a comforting arm around his shoulder. 'Don't worry, mate, we will get you through this. One day you will look back on this time and see it as a lesson learned.'

It was at that moment that they heard the sound of a bell in the distance. Daniel knew that sound only too well. He shouted, 'That's the bell at the cottage.' The two cousins turned and sprinted the fifty yards back to the Chough as fast as they could. Fully expecting to see someone in the doorway when they reached the cottage, they were surprised to discover there was no one around when they got there. Luke walked up to the bell. Though it was a still evening, did he detect a slight swaying of the strap, or was it his imagination? He turned to Daniel. 'Someone is definitely playing silly buggers.'

It was then that they heard a voice shout, 'Bleddy Tuss.' As before, the voice came from the undergrowth that rose high above the cottage. Both Luke and Daniel peered into the blackness, but it was impossible to see.

Luke shouted into darkness. 'If you have something to tell me, try saying it to my face.'

His request was greeted with total silence. A good five minutes passed before they turned towards the cottage. As Daniel unlocked the front door, they heard a high-pitched cackling laugh erupt from the bushes above them.

The two cousins could only look at each other, shrug and shake their heads.

Before following Daniel into the cottage, Luke could not resist aiming one more shout into the inky blackness. 'Tosser!'

FIVE

A GRUDGE REVEALED

Mark Reid was already well into his second cup of coffee as he studied the GPS tracker. Even though he had stayed up late the previous evening, he had risen bright and early that morning, as he did not want to be caught napping by any surprise movement of Luke Sadler's car. He was pleased to see that the vehicle had remained stationary in Helston throughout the evening. He fully expected Luke to return to London sometime that day, but he needed to be in the right place at the right time when that happened. He was pinning his hopes on Daniel Felton being with him. He went to the kitchen and put on some toast. In his job as a private investigator there were far too many occasions when he felt he was representing the wrong side: sadly this case felt like one of them. He had taken an instant dislike to Joe Blades the moment he had set eyes on him. He wore far too much jewellery for one thing. Besides which, he had always found it difficult to trust any man who wore a wrist bracelet. He did not have to rely on his previous experience as a police officer to guess that he was a wrong 'un. What could he do? He did not feel great about it, but the money was good. It had been his decision to walk away from the force and there was no one else to blame. The bread popped out of the toaster.

*

Luke Sadler had slept well, but he had awoken early. Though the beer from the previous evening had left him feeling a little heavy-headed, a vigorous shower and a hot cup of tea had proved to be the perfect cure. His mind went back to the events of the night before. It had certainly been an interesting evening. It seemed pretty obvious that there existed a small pocket of local hostility towards him and Daniel being in the village. He needed to know why.

He popped his head into Daniel's bedroom; he was still deep in slumber. Deciding to let him sleep it off, he closed the door and went downstairs. He opened the front door and took a lungful of fresh coastal air. His eyes automatically looked towards the bell. He thought back to the conversation with the old men. Could it really have once been a part of an old pirate ship? It certainly looked ancient enough. Either way, he thought it was a great story. He looked towards the high ridge of bushes to his right. He calculated that they rose to about thirty feet at the highest point. From where Luke stood, it did not look possible that the moron who had shouted last night could have climbed to the top. There was obviously another way up there. Being careful to take the front-door key with him, he decided to explore.

As he walked towards the high street in the village, he noticed that there were already a few early risers going about their Friday morning business. He took some reassurance that the majority of them bid him a good morning or gave a friendly nod of greeting. His attention was also drawn to the police posters appealing for people to be on the lookout for the missing banjo and red rucksack. As he drew level with the Jolly Pirate pub, he noticed a small alley to his right. The entrance was partially obscured by a large hydrangea plant. Unless you were familiar with the area, it could easily have been missed. Luke decided to follow the route of the alley as it wound its way up behind the pub. He eventually came to a high point that overlooked the coastline. Getting his bearings, he soon worked out his position in relation to the Chough. Though there was plenty of thick foliage, he noticed a small clearing that directly overlooked the cottage. Looking directly downwards, it gave him a clear view of the frontage and the parked Fiat 500. He looked down at the ground directly beneath him. Not only was the grass area slightly trampled, but he also noticed a few cigarette stubs scattered around. He had no doubt that he had found the place where the shouter from the previous night had been standing. Soon after returning to the cottage, he was rousing Daniel with the promise of his speciality bacon sandwich and a cup of hot tea.

'So you definitely think it was the place where he was hiding?' Daniel asked, as he took a mouthful of tea.

'No doubt about it. Whoever it was must have seen us leave the pub.'

'It definitely sounded like the same voice from the other night.'

'Well, whoever it is, they're a coward. If they have a problem they should tell us to our face.'

'I suppose it probably solves the mystery of the early morning bell-ringing.'

Luke frowned questioningly. 'Highly likely, but what possible reason could there be that would make someone go to those lengths?'

Daniel agreed, 'It beats me.'

Luke picked up his mobile phone. 'Finish your breakfast. I need you to show me where I can get a decent signal. Kate will be expecting a call.'

Soon afterwards, they were both negotiating the steep hilly lane that led to the Norman church.

Nearing the top, a slightly breathless Luke turned to Daniel. 'Now, before I speak to Kate, have you thought anymore about Lauren?'

Daniel took some time thinking about his answer. 'I wanted to ring her before she came down here. That's of course assuming she still wants to see me.'

Luke tried some gentle persuasion. 'Why don't you ring her later today? Then maybe she can come down with us sometime next week.'

Daniel seemed to take an age before answering, 'OK.'

They had now reached the atmospheric little churchyard and were grateful to sit down on one of the ancient stone tombs. Though there was no sunlight, the air was mild and perfectly still. Luke gave a little cheer as his phone displayed a strong signal.

Kate picked up after two rings. 'Hello, pet, can't speak too long as I have a client due in a couple of minutes. How's Daniel?'

'He's doing OK. Did Lauren stay the night?'

'Yes, she came over about eight.'

'Was she good company?'

'Well, despite everything she made the effort. As you can imagine, she's not happy.'

'What did you tell her?'

'Just that Daniel needed to get away for a bit but he still wanted to be with her.'

'How did she take that?'

'Not great, to be honest. She wants to hear it from him.'

'Hopefully that might be very soon. I will tell you more when I get home tonight.'

'I've got to go, pet, my client's just come in. Love to you, drive carefully.'

'Will do, hun, see you tonight.'

Luke turned to Daniel. 'Well, the good news is Lauren still wants to talk to you. You have to do the rest.'

Daniel looked relieved. 'I really don't deserve her.'

Luke smiled. 'That's probably true, my old buddy, but in this life you have to be grateful for anything good that comes your way.'

They both stood up. Daniel noticed that the path continued towards a small gate at the end of the churchyard. 'Let's see where this leads to.'

Arriving at the gate, they noticed that the path passed through a couple of fields before looping back towards the coastal path. They decided to walk back to the cottage using this route. Halfway through the first field they saw a distant figure walking towards them. As they drew nearer they could see it was a man accompanied by a golden retriever. There was something familiar about the affable features. It was Reg Turner, the friendly publican.

'Hello, lads, great morning to be taking the air.'

Luke waved a hand at the coastline. 'I can think of worse places to take your dog for a walk.'

Daniel made a fuss of the dog. 'What's his name?'

'Rusty.'

Daniel continued to ruffle the dog's fur. 'He's a cracker.'

'He is that. I won't change him, that's for sure. You heading back to the cottage?'

Luke answered, 'Yes, we've just discovered this path.'

'This is my regular route. Rusty can find his way back with his eyes closed.' Reg looked back towards the cottage. His expression suddenly clouded as he turned to Daniel. 'I do apologise for young Ricky Carlyon last night – I should have served you first but I had my reasons.'

Daniel thought back to the incident. 'I really don't know what his problem is. Can you throw some light on it?'

Both the cousins moved forward with interest as Reg lowered his voice in a conspiratorial manner. 'Ricky's mum, Elsie, and Old Tom got quite close after his wife died. Not romantic, you understand, Tom was a good few years older than her. Ricky's dad had buggered off years ago, so it was more for companionship than anything. The thing is, Elsie had always loved the cottage and had sort of set her heart on living there if it ever became available.'

Luke was beginning to understand. 'So when it finally came on the market she was priced right out of it.'

'Exactly, it hit his mum hard. Ever since, Ricky, who can be an emotional bugger at the best of times, has taken it upon himself to declare war on the Emmets… it's what they call you lot in these parts.'

Daniel thought back to all the hostility. It all made sense. The fact that it was Ricky's mum who lost out made it all the more personal. 'I appreciate you telling us this, Reg, it explains a lot.'

Luke added a reassurance, 'Don't worry, Reg, it won't put us off coming in to get our ration of Tribute in the Pirate.'

Reg laughed. 'I'm glad to hear it.' Saying their goodbyes, the two cousins walked on towards the coastal path.

Once out of earshot, Luke declared, 'Well, that pretty much explains everything, I would say.' He thought back to the previous night in the pub. 'I take it you were talking about the tall, fair-haired bloke who was giving us the evil eye last night.'

'That's the one.' Daniel then stated what they were both thinking, 'It's got to be him who damaged the car and has been shouting the abuse. Would you agree?'

To Luke it seemed clear-cut. 'Well, what do you think? I mean, seriously?'

With all that they knew now, it did seem blindingly obvious that it was Carlyon who had been behind all the harassment. Luke looked at his watch. It was getting on for eleven o'clock. 'I've just got time to show you where he was shouting from last night, before you run me back to Helston.'

After eventually returning to the Chough, they were just about to drive back to Helston when the police car arrived.

Luke was putting his overnight bag in the boot of the Fiat when Sergeant Wilkins and PC Kent got out of the car.

Wilkins guessed the young man was the cousin he had spoken to on the phone a couple of days earlier. 'I take it you are Mr Sadler?'

Luke shut the car boot and turned around. 'That's correct.'

'I'm Sergeant Wilkins, we spoke the other day.'

'I remember, pleased to meet you, Officer.'

At that point Daniel came out of the cottage and locked the door.

Luke explained, 'Daniel's just about to run me back to Helston, my car is parked at the Strathallan Guest House.'

Wilkins turned to Daniel. 'Lucky we caught you in time, Mr Felton.'

Daniel looked concerned. 'Is there something wrong?'

Wilkins did his best to sound reassuring. 'It's just a bit of police business, Mr Felton. We would like you to give us a DNA sample back at the station, if that's OK with you. It's totally voluntary on your part but purely for elimination purposes. I think it would be a good thing for you to comply.'

Daniel hesitated and looked at Luke.

Luke knew that unless they were thinking of arresting him, Daniel was within his rights to refuse. But on the other hand, if it proved his innocence it was worth complying. 'I think you should agree, Daniel.'

Sandra Kent also offered some gentle encouragement: 'It will not take too long, just a quick swab test.'

Daniel finally nodded. 'OK, but I don't want to draw attention when we drive out of the village.'

Wilkins answered, 'Don't worry yourself about that. We will leave now and wait for you at the guest house if that suits you?'

Luke answered, 'Much appreciated, Officer. We'll see you there.'

The two cousins got into the Fiat as the police car drove off. Daniel let out an exasperated sigh. 'I cannot believe that they still think I've got something to do with it.'

Luke offered solace. 'Don't take it personally – they have a job to do. Hopefully this test will put you in the clear.' He added with a smile, 'Unless you're not telling me something?'

Daniel pulled a face of indignation. 'That's all I need, you beginning to doubt me as well.' He started the Fiat and pointed it in the direction of Helston.

*

It was getting on for late afternoon as Mark Reid carefully parked his car in a side street just off the Cromwell Road in Kensington. He could see from the GPS that Luke Sadler was now making his way through Hammersmith on the Talgarth Road. He was very much counting on Luke not being the only occupant in the car and that Daniel Felton was accompanying him. It had seemed a long time from when the GPS had first signalled that Luke Sadler was finally leaving Helston and heading back to London. It had not helped that Sadler had appeared to have run into some seriously heavy traffic on the M4. But now he appeared to be making good progress and was getting close. It was Reid's plan to stick close to Sadler as he made his way back through Central London. Deciding when the time was right, he started the car and took up position, waiting for Sadler's black Audi to come into view. When it finally appeared he had no trouble picking it out and, after allowing for a couple of extra vehicles to pass, pushed out into the main road and moved smoothly into Luke's slipstream. As the Audi had passed, he had been disappointed that he had failed to catch sight of Daniel Felton in the passenger seat. Reid initially consoled himself with the thought that he could well be laid out asleep on the back seat. It was only after they had passed through Marylebone and the area of Felton's bedsit that he began to get serious doubts. Even though it was now approaching six o'clock in the evening, it appeared that Sadler was heading towards his Hoxton estate agents.

*

Luke let out a huge sigh of relief as he pulled up outside his Hoxton office. Coming on top of his beery night out with Daniel, the tediously long drive home had left him feeling more than a little washed out. He had arranged to pick up Kate from work on his way home. He got out of the car and was enjoying a good stretch, when Kate hurriedly exited the office and locked the door. 'I was wondering whether you were ever going to get here.' She gave him a quick kiss on the cheek.

Luke handed her the car keys. 'You can do the honours, hun, I'm just about knackered.'

She looked at him. 'You do look a bit rough. Sure it's not a case of too much beer?'

Luke laughed. 'I must admit, it was an interesting night. I've plenty to tell you.'

'I look forward to hearing about it.' Kate made her way round to the driver's side. It was just as she was getting into the car that she caught a glimpse of an occupied Ford Fiesta parked across the road. It was dark and she could not even begin to guess the colour, but there was something familiar about it. She had a strong feeling that it was not the first time she had seen it. She was just about to mention this to Luke when the cars headlights came on and the car moved swiftly away.

She turned to Luke. 'I'm sure I've seen that car before.'

Luke had been too tired to pay much attention. 'What car?'

Kate pointed at the taillights that were disappearing in the distance. 'That one there.' Noticing she was not getting much response, she glanced across at Luke's weary features and shook her head. 'Never mind, pet, I think it's time we got you home.'

Luke adjusted the passenger seat and closed his eyes. 'Sounds good to me.'

*

Daniel Felton sat down on one of the old tombstones in front of the old parish church and looked at his phone. The signal was strong and there were no excuses. It was now or never if he was going to ring Lauren. It had been a strange day. The publican's revelation about Ricky Carlyon's mum had gone a long way to explain Ricky's open hostility. Was Ricky the shouter from the bushes and the culprit who'd damaged the car? It certainly looked that way and Luke seemed convinced. He thought fondly of his cousin. Where would he be without him? Up the creek without a paddle would not cover it. He was a true diamond. And then there had been the trip to Helston Police Station for the DNA swab test. The process had not taken long, and both Sergeant Wilkins and PC Kent had been very polite, but he had found the whole experience intimidating just the same. Hopefully that would be the last of it.

He looked up at the early evening sky. The fading light was tinged with a pink glow that illuminated the horizon, and the air was still and peaceful in the churchyard. He looked around him appreciatively. The Norman church had a traditional square bell tower with a clock, surrounded by leaning tombstones mottled with lichen. He liked it here; it gave him time to think. He looked at his phone and scrolled through the contact list. He found Lauren's name.

It rang several times before Lauren picked up. 'Where are you?'

Daniel felt himself hesitate for a second. It felt so good to hear her voice. 'I'm in Cornwall, one of Luke's properties.'

'I suppose you were eventually going to tell me what the hell's going on.'

Daniel could certainly sense a bit of attitude coming

down the line. This was not going to be easy. Why should it be? 'I'm so sorry. I got myself in a mess and I didn't want to drag you into it.'

'That's what upsets me. The fact you felt you couldn't tell me.'

'The truth was I felt ashamed that I've got myself in such a hole. I thought you would split with me anyway if I told you.'

There was a brief silence before Lauren spoke again. 'Are you going to enlighten me?'

Daniel steeled himself. 'Well, you know I used to dabble in the online gambling.'

Lauren recalled that there had been irritating occasions in the past when he would bury his head in the screen for hours. She had a good idea what was coming. 'Yes?'

'Well, it sort of took over my life. For reasons I can't explain, it became the most important thing in my day. I could not stop thinking about it.'

Lauren guessed the rest. 'So you have got yourself into massive debt.'

Daniel felt a slight catch in his voice. 'Yes.'

Lauren felt a flood of mixed emotions: betrayal, anger, pity. But surprisingly there was something else. Irrational as it seemed in that moment, she realised she still loved him in spite of everything. She heard herself saying, 'When can I see you?'

Daniel felt the clouds lifting as he eagerly answered, 'As soon as you can get down here. Luke said you could come down with him next week.'

'I will probably have to get a couple of days off work.'

Daniel felt a burst of emotion. 'I can't wait to see you. I'll make it up to you, I promise.'

Lauren's response was more measured. 'We'll have to take it a day at a time and see where we end up.'

Daniel reined himself in. 'Of course, it's on your terms.'

'Hope to see you next week.'

'Look forward to it.' As Daniel walked back down the hill towards the village, he could not remember the last time he had felt such a spring in his step. Things were looking up.

But he had not been alone. Somebody at the far end of the churchyard emerged furtively from behind a large stone pillar and watched him leave.

*

Mark Reid was sitting in his car outside his flat. His calculation that Daniel Felton would have returned from Cornwall with his cousin had come up with the wrong answer. It had been a disappointing setback, but nothing more. He picked up his iPhone and began to surf the various property websites associated with Luke Sadler. He whistled softly as he browsed through the fashionable studio flats and three-storey townhouses on display. One thing he knew for sure: they were way out of his league. He would have struggled to have afforded the door knocker on most of them.

He was about to log out when a website called 'Sadler Horizons' caught his eye. It was advertising a couple of holiday homes situated on the Dorset coast. He could not help being impressed. It seemed Luke had also been branching out into the holiday market. His attention was drawn to a heading titled 'Holiday Cottage Coming Soon'. He felt his detecting juices start to flow as he digested the detail. The Chough Cottage, Tregarris, Cornwall. This looked very promising. He quickly looked up Tregarris on his mobile phone map. There it was – a small village just a few miles south of Helston. Of course, there was the possibility that Sadler had travelled down there purely on business, but his well-honed investigative instincts told him differently. He was prepared to wager a good sum that he would find Daniel Felton holed up in the village somewhere; the Chough cottage seemed a good place to start looking. At that moment, the idea of spending a few days down in Cornwall did not seem unattractive. It presented a good opportunity for him to change his scene for a while. He could not remember the last time he had visited that part of the world. He rang Joe Blades to tell him his plans.

One hour later he was sitting in his favourite local Indian restaurant, contemplating an early morning start for his journey to Cornwall. He had just finished his madras and was now cooling down with a refreshing glass of Cobra lager. He had always liked his Indian food nice and hot. It used to be a running joke with his wife. Unless it made his fillings sizzle it was not worth the effort or the price. He sighed. They used to laugh in those days. He struggled to remember exactly when the laughter had stopped. He decided that it would be prudent if he stayed outside Tregarris, so he had booked a few nights at the Strathallan, in Helston. *If it's good enough for Luke Sadler*, he reasoned to himself. He was quite looking forward to it. He thought back to the incident with Sadler's girlfriend outside the estate agents earlier on. Though it had been dark and he had been parked some way up the road, he was sure she had been staring. He hadn't hung around to find out if he was correct in his suspicion. That was probably another good reason to get out of London for a few days. He finished off his lager and asked for the bill.

*

'Well, I guess that puts young Felton in the clear.' Jack Wilkins was studying the results of the DNA test that had just come in from the lab in Penzance.

DI Everett still did not sound totally convinced. 'As far as the cigarette butts are concerned, yes. Of course, there is still the possibility that the burns were inflicted on Fraser before the assault that killed him.'

Wilkins had to concede that the rate that Duncan Fraser cultivated enemies, they could not totally rule it out. They were working late at the police station and were finishing off a pizza that Sandra Kent had ordered in earlier. Wilkins answered, 'I suppose we can't totally rule out that the butts could have been dropped quite innocently by anyone walking along the coastal path.'

Everett swallowed his last mouthful of pizza. 'Exactly, they might have nothing whatsoever to do with the burns found on Fraser's neck.'

Sandra Kent was thinking back to her conversations with the locals in Tregarris. They had been very eager to talk about the murder and give their opinions. In her experience it was usually the people who didn't talk that had something to hide in tight-knit communities. But maybe with just the correct amount of financial encouragement that could change. She posed the question. 'Do you think it could be worth putting out a reward for anyone who might be willing to squeal for a price?'

Everett looked interested. 'That's definitely something we might have to think about.' He gave Sandra a look of approval as he got up to leave. 'I like your way of thinking.'

Kent felt a slight blush developing. It was not often she received praise from anyone, let alone from Martin Everett.

After Everett had left the office, Jack Wilkins looked across at her and grinned. 'Well, that's got to be the highlight of your day, a compliment from DI Everett.'

Kent laughed. 'I will have to put that in my calendar.'

Wilkins face turned serious. 'He's not wrong, though, a reward could be just what's needed to get the answers in this case.'

'My old boss in Salisbury Central always used to say that getting information in the underworld was like squeezing a pip from an orange: you just had to get the right angle.'

Wilkins found himself nodding in agreement. 'Well, three cheers for your old boss.'

Kent laughed and rose from her desk. 'Let's have another cuppa.'

Wilkins did his best to impersonate DI Everett. 'I like your way of thinking.'

*

Three hundred miles away in a small office in Soho, a dim light burned into the early hours. Joe Blades sat at his desk opposite his two heavies, Vince and Max. He was informing them of Mark Reid's revelations regarding Daniel Felton. 'We don't want to let go of this one very easily. If we play the situation correctly with this devoted, wealthy cousin, there's a chance it could prove to be highly lucrative for all of us. Bear in mind that if, as I expect, Mr Reid eventually discovers Felton's bolthole in Cornwall, it will probably mean a trip down there for you two.'

The two men looked at each other before Vince answered, 'Whatever it takes, boss, you just point us in the right direction.'

'Hopefully I will have more detail for you after the weekend.'

It was Vince that spoke once more. 'Just to be clear, when you say don't let go of this one easily, I take it you mean some heavy leaning?'

There was no hesitation from Joe Blades. 'You have never let me down before, Vince. I will rely on your good judgement. Do what you feel is necessary.'

A malicious grin began to form around the mouth of the one they called Max.

SIX

A CHILLING FABLE

Luke Sadler was sitting quietly in the corner of the Benugo coffee shop in Wigmore Street. Thinking he might have to pay off some of Daniel's debts in person, he had risen early that morning and took the tube into Central London. Making use of the free Wi-Fi in the shop, he had already made good progress in settling the accounts of the numerous organisations and individuals asking Daniel for their money back. Some of the bank transfers had amounted to some tidy sums, but he was now trawling through the various friends and acquaintances where the debts were more modest.

It was a late Saturday morning and he calculated that he still had thirty minutes or so before the normal lunchtime stampede for snacks and takeaways. As it was, he was appreciating the calmer atmosphere in the shop, giving him time to focus. He was familiar with some of the names that cropped up in Daniel's phone: people he had been introduced to at various times when he and Daniel had met up on social occasions. There was one name in particular that he knew quite well… John Cameron. It seemed that Daniel still owed him thirty pounds. As he recalled, he lived on the same street as Daniel.

Luke dialled the number. It rang only once before it was answered by an excited voice. 'Hello, Daniel. Am I glad to hear from you!'

Luke let him down gently. 'Sorry to disappoint you, John, but it's Luke, his cousin.'

Now there was a trace of alarm in the voice. 'Has something happened to Daniel?'

Luke was quick to reassure him. 'No, nothing like that, Daniel's perfectly fine.'

There was an audible sigh of relief. 'Thank God for that! I have been really worried about him. Lauren has been asking me if I knew where he was.'

'The truth is, John, he did hit a bit of trouble, but it's all sorted now. He will probably tell you everything in his own good time.'

'Give him my best. I'm so glad to hear he is still in one piece. Last week there were these two men asking after him and they looked like they could do a bit of damage.'

Now it was Luke's turn to sound interested. 'You saw them?'

'Yes, they approached me outside the pub last week. I didn't like the look of them so I played it dumb. The next thing I hear is Lauren telling me he's done a runner. I thought it best not to tell her about the two men; she sounded pretty frantic as it was.'

Luke was relieved to hear that. The situation was

stressful enough for her as it was. He asked, 'That was the only time you have seen them?'

John Cameron thought back to the two menacing individuals. 'Yes, hopefully it will be the one and only time.'

Luke changed the subject. 'Anyway, I have some good news for you. I believe that Daniel owed you thirty quid.'

'That's right, but I'm not waiting on it. I'm just glad he's OK.'

'Well, Daniel wants to get it back to you. Give us your bank details and it'll be there in a jiffy.'

There was some token resistance before John Cameron obliged and Luke completed the transfer. Soon after finishing the call, Luke noticed the coffee shop was starting to get busy. He scanned Daniel's phone one more time. There were just a couple of names remaining to be contacted. The time in the shop had been very productive, but now it was time to leave.

*

The sun was shining brightly in Tregarris, and though the air was crisp, there was still a degree of warmth in the late autumn sunshine. Gazing out at the sweeping view of the Cornish coastline, Reg Turner took in a lungful of fresh air, as his dog Rusty ran on ahead of him. It was on glorious days like this that he would not have wanted to have been anywhere else in the world. He was making his way back across the fields towards the Norman church, with his golden retriever leading the way. He had now been the proprietor of the Jolly Pirate for the best part of ten years, but he never tired of the views and the Cornish way of life. Moving down to Tregarris from Bournemouth had been the best move he had ever made. It was just a shame that Dorothy had never felt the same way. Even before the illness that so tragically took her away, she had never settled… God bless her.

He passed through the churchyard and started making his way down the steep path that led to the village. He had momentarily lost sight of Rusty, but that was not unusual, as he would often disappear into the various nooks and crannies that were so familiar to him. Halfway down the path, Reg heard a rustling in the bushes to his right. Unusually he had to call out Rusty's name more than once, before the retriever eventually emerged from the bush with something clasped tightly in his jaws. Initially, Reg had some trouble prising the object out of Rusty's mouth. It looked to be the tatty burnt remains of what appeared to be a satchel. On closer examination, he could just detect a hint of red colouring on one of the scorched straps. Reg suddenly gave a small gasp of comprehension. It looked like his dog had found Duncan Fraser's missing rucksack.

*

Daniel Felton strode out purposefully along the coastal path. The sun was shining brightly, and the sea and sky were giving a vivid blue backdrop to the small coves and hidden beaches he was discovering along the way. He had been walking for just over an hour in a westerly direction and had now reached Trewavas Head. He decided it was a good point to have a rest and take in the view. He sat down on a rocky boulder that looked out over a blue and infinite sea. He was feeling better already. He reached into his holdall and pulled out a bottle of water and a Mars bar. He was glad he had made the decision to have a good walk, rather than stay back in the cottage viewing more breakfast TV.

Disappointingly, he had endured another restless night. Not only had his earlier conversation with Lauren left him in a state of eager anticipation of what was to come, but also the bell had rung once again in the early hours. This time he had not gone to the window when the bell sounded. Instead he had chosen to ignore it and buried his head under the bedclothes. Thinking back to it now, he was not totally sure why. At the time he had justified his inaction by thinking he would not give young Carlyon the satisfaction. But being honest with himself, he was still disturbed by the recollection of the misty image that had formed a couple of nights before. Luke pointing out the creepy coincidence with the stopped grandfather clock had certainly not helped. If, as it was beginning to look like, the nocturnal prankster really was Ricky Carlyon, what was so significant about three o'clock in the morning? He looked out onto the coastline and his thoughts went once more to Lauren. He could hardly wait to share this coastline with her. The thought of it made him feel happy.

*

'It looks like it was about here.' Jack Wilkins was down on his haunches examining the blackened patch of grass where a fire had once burned. He and Sandra Kent had not wasted much time in getting to Tregarris, after the phone call from the publican of the Jolly Pirate. Reg Turner had shown them the spot where Rusty had emerged with the burnt rucksack, and they had now squeezed through the bush into a small clearing on the other side.

Kent was holding a forensic bag containing what appeared to be the charred remains of Duncan Fraser's rucksack. Her eyes were keenly scanning the ground surrounding the area. 'It looks like there might be some good footprints for crime scene to examine.'

Jack Wilkins nodded. 'I think we should get the boys out here right away.' He radioed in to headquarters and requested some forensic officers.

Sandra pointed to a couple of cigarette stubs lying nearby. 'Be interesting to know whether the DNA matches the stubs found on the coastal path.'

Wilkins looked at them with interest. 'It would go some way to confirming that our man is a torturer if they do.' He pointed to the bag in Sandra's hand containing the blackened rucksack. 'I think it could be the right time to take up your suggestion and get out a reward. I reckon a sum of about five thousand would do it.'

Sandra looked pleased. 'Let's see if we can squeeze that pip.'

*

Martin Everett turned up the volume on his car radio. 'Wonderwall' by Oasis had always been one of his favourites. He could not help emitting a sigh. Now in his early forties, he was at the stage where he was beginning to lament the passing of his youth. Had the Britpop phenomenon really been over twenty years ago? Time was passing far too quickly for his liking.

He was on his way to the Helston HQ in Godolphin Street, after being informed about the discovery of the remains of the missing rucksack. The fact it was found in Tregarris was significant; potentially it seemed to narrow the field. It looked highly likely they were looking for someone living in or around the village. In theory, this still did not rule out young Felton. He knew that Wilkins and PC Kent were not convinced, but he still felt there was something about the young Londoner's story that did not quite add up.

He turned the car into Market Place. It was a fine Saturday afternoon in Helston, and there were a fair number of local shoppers who had been tempted outside by the sunny autumn weather. As he slowed to allow some pedestrians to cross the road, he let out a gasp of recognition. He was sure the familiar figure passing in front of him was one of his old senior constables from his days in the Met. More mature and portly than he remembered, but he was sure it was definitely him. What was his name? Mark… Ross… Reece… Reid. That was it, Mark Reid. He quickly pulled over and wound down the driver's window. 'Mark Reid?'

Mark Reid could not help recoiling in surprise. He had not long booked into the Strathallan Guest House after arriving just after midday. Now stretching his legs after the long journey down from London, he had been enjoying a leisurely stroll around the town streets. The last person he would have expected to bump into was one of his old colleagues from his days in the Met. He recognised

Martin Everett immediately. He had been one of the eager young constables he had taken under his wing back in the nineties. He approached the car window. 'I don't believe it! Martin Everett, if I'm not mistaken?'

Everett looked delighted. 'It's been a long time. What are you doing here?'

'Just taking a few days' break.'

Everett remembered he'd been married. 'Where's the trouble and strife?'

Reid adopted a pained expression. 'Oh, it's a long story. The bottom line is we're no longer together.'

Everett had a distant memory of Reid once proudly introducing his wife on one occasion. He remembered her being a cheerful sort. 'I'm sorry to hear that, Mark.'

Reid shrugged. 'These things happen.'

'Are you still working?'

Reid looked a bit defensive. 'I took an early retirement from the force.' He saw a look of surprise flash across Everett's face. He added quickly, 'I still keep my hand in with some private work.'

Everett found it hard to keep the disappointment out of his voice. 'You are a private investigator?'

Reid tried to sound upbeat. 'It keeps me ticking over.'

Everett handed over a card with his contact details. 'Well, all I can say is the Met is all the poorer for losing good men like you. You taught me a lot, Mark. Be great to catch up over a pint if you get the time.'

Reid looked at the card. 'I'll do that.'

Everett gave a genial wave and drove away.

*

Daniel Felton had a good feeling as he walked back towards the cottage. The combination of a walk in the fine weather and the thought of seeing Lauren had engendered that feel-good factor. Remembering that his food supplies were running a little low, he decided to walk on through the village towards the convenience store. As he passed the entrance to the lane that led up to the churchyard, he caught a glimpse of Ricky Carlyon talking to two other people. It had only been a brief glance, but he was sure one of them had been a girl. He could not be sure if the other one was the youth he had seen arguing with Carlyon in the lane a few days before. He thought no more of it, but on his way back from the store he was certain that he recognised the same girl standing outside the Jolly Pirate, looking straight at him. Something about her expression made him feel distinctly uncomfortable. There was no sign of Carlyon. After walking on some distance, he took a peek back over his shoulder. There she was: still standing there, staring.

*

'We think we should pitch it at about £5,000,' Jack Wilkins suggested to DI Everett as he glanced across to Sandra Kent for support.

Everett waved him away with a dismissive hand. 'Far too high, the powers that be would never go for it – £2,500 is a more realistic number.'

They were all assembled in the police station discussing the implications of the discovered rucksack.

Sandra sounded a bit disappointed. 'Well, either way, I think it's a good time to launch it.'

Everett nodded in agreement. 'That's a useful sum of money, should be more than enough to tempt someone.'

Wilkins smiled. 'Poor old Rusty didn't even get a bone.'

Everett gave a chuckle and sat down at his desk. 'It was a lucky break, him finding it, that's for sure.' He had a good feeling that they were closing in. 'Whoever burnt that rucksack is gonna feel pretty uncomfortable when the news of its discovery gets out there.'

Wilkins thought of the cigarette stubs. 'We should get the results from forensic anytime. If the DNA on the stubs matches those found near Fraser's body, we'll know a lot more about the nature of the beast we're after.'

Everett almost looked pleased. 'It will mean we probably have a sadistic torturer on our hands.'

Sandra pulled a face but decided not to comment.

Everett motioned as if he was winding in a fish. 'Get the reward notices out as quickly as possible – I think I am going to enjoy reeling in this whopper.'

Sandra Kent answered, 'I'll get on it right away, sir.'

Thirty minutes later, the results from the forensic report were on Everett's desk. After a few minutes' scrutiny, he looked up. 'Well, that confirms it. We are looking for a sadistic torturer who smokes like a chimney.'

Wilkins commented, 'That could go some way in narrowing down the search. Nowadays a heavy smoker tends to attract more attention than once was the case.'

Everett studied the report closely. 'Unfortunately the footprints found around the burnt ground were not distinctive enough. Let's think about this. There is no record of this DNA on our database. Yet whoever did this is one nasty piece of work. What does that suggest to you, Jack?'

'Either someone who has offended before but up to now has never been lifted, or someone just starting out, someone fairly young.'

'Exactly. I think we can narrow the search down to someone who is a chain smoker, probably a young man living in the area.'

'We'll make a start drilling down into the local community.'

'Good man.' Martin Everett looked at his watch. 'Fancy a pint in the Anchor on the way home tonight, Jack?'

The Blue Anchor in Coinagehall Street served real ale and was one of Everett's favourite watering holes. It was not unknown for him to offer the occasional invite to his Sergeant when the mood was upon him.

Jack Wilkins hesitated for a brief second before answering, 'Oh, go on then.'

*

Mark Reid was well into his second pint of Spingo. The landlord had sold it to him as one of the oldest real ales in Cornwall, and he was enjoying every drop. He looked around his surroundings approvingly. The Blue Anchor was an old medieval inn, just around the corner from the Strathallan Guest House. Now sitting in its cosy bar in front of an open fire, he was feeling he had made the correct decision in entering its ancient interior. He had already decided to put off his visit to Tregarris until the morning. As far as he was concerned the whereabouts of Daniel Felton could wait a little longer.

He thought back to his encounter with Martin Everett earlier that day. Seeing him after all these years had given him a bit of a jolt. It took him back to a happier time when his life seemed to have more meaning and purpose. He remembered Everett as being one of his brightest young constables, and almost from day one they had formed a mutual respect. He recalled, with regret, the flicker of disappointment he had seen pass across Everett's face when he had told him he was now doing private work. The thought that he had gone down in the estimation of a former colleague made him feel ashamed. It was also a painful reminder of just how far his life had dipped since those halcyon days.

After glancing at his watch, he hurriedly finished off his pint. He was booked for an evening meal in the Strathallan and he was feeling hungry. He rose from his seat and walked through the narrow corridor that led out onto the street. It was then that he bumped right into Martin Everett and Jack Wilkins entering the inn.

Everett again looked delighted to see him. 'Twice in one day, Mark. I think someone's trying to tell us something.'

Reid had again been caught by surprise, but he quickly regained his composure. 'Hi, Martin, it's good to see you again.'

Everett gestured towards the inn interior. 'Been sampling the local ales?'

Reid smiled. 'I can recommend the Spingo, that's for sure.'

Everett laughed. 'You are preaching to the converted, my friend. Can you stay for another?'

Reid put his hands up in apology. 'Sorry, Martin, I'm booked for a meal at the Strathallan.'

Everett looked disappointed. 'Shame, another time, perhaps.' He introduced him to his sergeant before adding, 'This man was one of the Metropolitan's finest, Jack.'

Wilkins could sense the warmth that still existed between the two men. 'Pleased to meet you, Mark.'

Reid held out a hand. 'Hope he is treating you well, Sarge, I taught him everything he knows so you can blame me.'

'I've no complaints – well, none that I can say in front of him,' Wilkins replied.

Everett pulled an expression of mock indignation. 'I take it you still want that pint, Jack?' He turned back to Reid. 'Remember, Mark, you have my number.'

'Don't worry, I won't forget.'

Everett watched Reid walk away. He looked a lot shabbier than he remembered. Age and the divorce had obviously taken its toll. He now looked every inch the archetypal private eye. A thought suddenly occurred to him. Could it be that he was not really on holiday and that he was down here in Cornwall on a job? It was to be this intriguing possibility that occupied his thoughts as he buried his nose into his first pint of Spingo.

*

Mark Reid stood looking down the hill that led into Tregarris. He had been grateful to find a small space to park his car at the entrance to the village. With his eyes keenly taking in every detail, he started to make his way down the hill. Considering it was out of season and fast approaching Sunday lunchtime, there seemed to be plenty of people milling about the place. He was surprised to see a young policewoman on the other side of the street that appeared to be conducting an enquiry. Was it his imagination or did he detect a slight buzz of excitement about the place? He got his answer when he stopped and studied a police poster. In bold print, it was offering a financial reward for information regarding the murder of a man found dead on the coastal path. Reid shook his head in wonder; clearly there was more that went on in Cornish villages than he imagined. He nodded genially to a young man standing outside the Jolly Pirate who was drawing deeply on a cigarette. He guessed he was a member of the kitchen staff, as he was wearing a black and white checked apron. His friendly gesture was greeted with a scowl and barely acknowledged. Reid made a mental note: not all the natives were necessarily amicable.

He had studied the village on Google Maps, so he was familiar with the layout and already knew the location of the Chough cottage. He walked on to the end of the street and made his way to the coastal path. He soon came to the cottage on his left-hand side. There was a white Fiat parked outside. He felt ninety-nine per cent sure that he had found Daniel Felton's bolthole. It only remained for him to get a positive sighting. Fortuitously, he did not have to wait too long. As if he had mentally summoned him up, there was Daniel approaching him from the direction of the coastal path. Despite the fact that he was wearing a parka with the collar pulled up, Reid recognised him almost immediately. Daniel barely gave Reid a glance as he bid him good morning and walked on past the cottage and into the village. Reid turned and followed at a discreet distance as he watched him stop and enter the Jolly Pirate. Reid allowed himself a smirk of satisfaction. His hunch had paid off and he had found his prey; he just needed the final confirmation that Daniel was staying in Chough cottage.

*

'Pint of Tribute, Reg.' It was just approaching twelve o'clock on the Sunday lunchtime and the Jolly Pirate was practically empty as the staff prepared themselves for the traditional midday rush. Daniel had just returned from his invigorating coastal walk and felt he had earned his pint.

Reg took his time as he pulled at the pump with practised expertise. He looked pleased to see Daniel. 'You're my first customer today, Mr Felton.'

Danny raised his glass and took a long swill of the refreshing beer. 'It's lively but delicious,' he said appreciatively, before wiping the white foam from his lips.

Reg leaned his elbows on the bar. 'Did you hear about how clever Rusty was yesterday?'

Daniel looked blank. 'No, have I missed something?'

'Were you not in here last night? Everyone was talking about it.'

'No, I decided to have a quiet night in with the TV. Why, what have I missed?'

'Only the tale of Rusty and the rucksack, that's all. We were out on our walk yesterday and Rusty went and found the murdered man's rucksack.'

Daniel remembered catching a glimpse of PC Kent on the high street as he had entered the pub: this would explain it. 'Really, whereabouts did he find it?'

'It was behind a hedge in the lane that leads up to the church.'

'Who has it now?'

'The police have got it. It was in a right state. It looked like whoever it was tried to burn the evidence.'

Something stirred vaguely in Daniel's memory but he couldn't quite put his finger on it. He grinned. 'Good old Rusty. Does he get a reward?'

'Unfortunately not, though funnily enough there is now a reward of £2,500 for anyone who can name the guilty party. Did you not see the posters outside?'

'No, I must have had my beer glasses on. By the time I got to the end of my walk, I only had eyes for one of your foaming pints.' Daniel whistled softly. 'Two and a half grand is a tidy sum.'

Reg looked a little excited. 'I will have to get my thinking cap on.'

Daniel laughed. 'Have you got a deerstalker?'

Reg grinned back. 'You can be my Watson.'

Talk of mysteries brought a sudden thought to Daniel. He signalled for the landlord to come closer. 'Changing the subject completely, Reg, was there anything strange about old Tom's death?'

Reg's face turned serious. 'Why do you ask?'

'Well, the other night one of his old mates went to say

something and the other one firmly stopped him in his tracks.'

A knowing grin passed across Reg's face. 'Oh, that'd be about the Black Dragon's bell.'

Daniel wanted to know more. 'The old pirate ship, what about it?'

'Well, Bill and Alf are convinced that Tom was killed by the old pirate Red Robbo. According to them, Tom was being bothered by the bell being rung in the early hours.'

Daniel again felt the hairs on his neck start to rise.

Reg went on. 'Tom lived in the real world and didn't believe a word of the old seaman's yarn. He told them he was going to confront whoever was ringing the bell the next time it happened. Next thing they know, Tom is found dead in his doorway one morning, struck down by a massive heart attack. I've tried to tell them it was natural causes, but they won't hear anything different. As far as they're concerned, Red Robbo and the crew of the Black Dragon returned in the night and slaughtered old Tom.'

Daniel felt distinctly uncomfortable. 'You have to admit, it's a grisly tale.'

Reg nodded. 'And that's all it is. But Bill and Alf, they just love a ghost story and they've convinced themselves it's true.'

There was a brief moment when Daniel thought of telling Reg of his own experiences with the bell, but then thought better of it. What would be the point? Reg would probably think he was going mad. Besides, it was bound to be young Ricky Carlyon playing tricks.

Instead he finished his pint and said, 'Have another pint with me, Reg, we'll drink to Old Tom and Rusty.'

Reg looked more than grateful. 'Don't mind if I do, young Daniel, don't mind if I do.'

SEVEN

BACK IN THE FRAME

Jenna Truscott watched the young policewoman from across the street. There had already been numerous occasions when she had gone to approach her, only to change her mind at the last minute. She knew that what she was about to do was wrong, but she loved him and he said he needed her help. He had made a promise that he would be her boyfriend if she did what he asked. The thought of what it would feel like to be his girlfriend had filled her every waking moment. Now she just had to find the courage to go through with it. She steeled herself one more time, before walking towards the policewoman.

Sandra Kent was busily making herself known in the tight-knit community of Tregarris. With the discovery of the burnt rucksack and the offer of the reward, there seemed no better time to strike while the iron was hot. She had felt this so strongly, that she had even volunteered to put in some extra hours on a Sunday. So far she hadn't had much luck with her enquiries, but she did feel her personable high profile on the high street was beginning to break down some barriers with the locals. While she had been conducting her interviews, she had become increasingly aware that a young girl seemed to be hovering nearby. At first she had thought that she was just being curious, but it became obviously apparent by her body language that she was waiting for the right moment to approach her. Sure enough, that moment eventually arrived.

'Can I help you?'

The girl seemed nervous and very hesitant. 'I think I saw someone carrying the rucksack.'

Sandra felt a stirring of interest as she opened her notebook. 'Where was this?'

The girl answered in a monotone voice. 'It was in the lane where the rucksack was found, the one that leads to the church.'

'What day was this?'

'I can't remember exactly, sometime last week.'

Sandra Kent asked the obvious question. 'Did you recognise this person?'

The girls face was almost expressionless as she answered instantly, 'Yes, it was the boy that's staying in the Chough.'

Sandra's pencil hovered over her notebook. 'You are definitely sure about this?'

The girl nodded eagerly. 'Yes, it was definitely him. He was holding something red close to his body.'

Sandra Kent studied the young girl's features closely. It was not an attractive face. 'You are sure it was the rucksack?'

The girl continued in a stilted tone, as if she was reading from a script. 'At the time I didn't think much of it. It was only when I heard that the rucksack was found near the church yesterday, that I thought back to the boy in the lane and remembered him carrying something red. I'm sure it was the rucksack.'

'What's your name?'

'Jenna Truscott.'

'Address?'

'Thirty Fisherman's Hill.'

Sandra wrote down the details in her notebook. 'OK, Miss Truscott, I'll probably need to come back to you at some stage.'

Jenna Truscott hardly made eye contact as she nodded, before walking away swiftly. Sandra watched her go. She was far from convinced that the girl was telling the truth. If her first impressions were correct, either the girl had made up the story in a misguided attempt to get some part of the financial reward or, more significantly, she was skewing the enquiry away from the real culprit. Either way the girl could end up in serious trouble. Her thoughts turned once more to Daniel Felton. Why did everything keep coming back to him?

*

'So you were not totally convinced that Jenna Truscott's testimony was reliable?' It was Monday morning in Helston HQ and DI Everett was scanning through the various statements obtained by his constable from the day before.

Sandra Kent pulled a face. 'The girl's whole manner seemed like she was acting out a part. To be honest, without sounding unkind, she didn't seem to be the whole ticket.'

Everett looked up. 'In what way exactly?'

Sandra cast her mind back to the girl's face and attitude. She remembered Jenna's expressionless features and oddly cold body language. 'I would be surprised if there is not some intellectual disability in her background.'

Everett nodded in comprehension. 'I see. Of course, it doesn't necessarily mean her statement is any less worthy.'

'I realise that. It's just that her whole story felt so contrived.'

Everett made a decision. 'I think the time has come for me to take a look at young Daniel Felton. Where this case is concerned he is like a bad smell that keeps coming back. I think we'll pay him a visit this afternoon so I can run my eye over him.'

There was the faint hint of disappointment in Kent's voice as she answered, 'OK, sir.'

Everett picked up on her tone. 'I know you're not convinced about Felton, Sandra, but you have to admit that his name keeps cropping up in this affair.'

She reluctantly agreed. 'I can't deny that.'

Everett turned to Jack Wilkins, who had been sitting at his desk listening to the exchange. 'We'll take a trip into Tregarris after lunch and surprise him.'

*

A heavy rain was falling from a slate-grey sky when Everett and Jack Wilkins arrived at the Chough. The car splashed up water from the rapidly deepening puddles, as Everett brought the car to a halt outside. Everett's shrewd eye was eager to take in every detail of his surroundings as he walked towards the cottage. He paused and studied the large brass bell that hung by the door. 'That's something you don't see every day,' he remarked, before giving the rope a firm tug. In order to surprise Daniel and turn up unannounced, they had taken a gamble that he had not ventured out in the horrible weather. Their judgement had proven correct, with Daniel promptly appearing at the door.

Everett introduced himself, while all the time taking in his first impressions of the clean-cut young man standing before him. 'Would be much appreciated, Mr Felton, if we can take up a few minutes of your time.'

Daniel found it difficult to disguise his surprise and anxiety as he invited the two policemen inside. He had hoped he had seen the last of them. He attempted to regain his composure. 'Would you like a drink?'

Everett politely turned down the offer, as he wanted to quickly cut to the chase. 'How much longer do you plan to stay in Tregarris, Mr Felton?'

It occurred to Daniel that up to now he had not given it much thought, so relieved had he been just to get away from his situation in London. 'I cannot say exactly, maybe a couple more weeks,' he answered uncertainly.

Everett could immediately see that there was a nervousness about Daniel that suggested he was hiding something, even though his apparent willingness to hang around Tregarris did not suggest the actions of a guilty man. Everett applied a little subtle pressure by deliberately extending the silence that followed the young man's answer.

Daniel sounded a little agitated. 'Why are you interested? Was my DNA test not conclusive?'

Everett chose to reassure him on that point. 'No worries there, Mr Felton, you were as clean as a whistle. It's just that we have since had some further information relating to the rucksack that was found in Tregarris on Saturday.'

Daniel was baffled. 'What sort of information?' he asked anxiously.

Everett did not hold back. 'We have a witness who says they saw you carrying the rucksack towards the area where it was found.'

Daniel could not help raising his voice. 'That's complete rubbish! Whoever said that is either mistaken or they're lying.'

Everett found his answer interesting. 'Why would someone lie about that, Mr Felton?'

Daniel thought immediately of Ricky Carlyon, but surely even his open hostility would not stretch to putting him in the frame for a murder? One thing for sure, he would have to be certain in his own mind before naming him to the police. He finally answered under Everett's withering gaze. 'I have no idea. I don't deny that I walk up that lane sometimes. It's the only place where you can get a decent phone signal.'

Everett gave him a steady stare. 'The witness seemed pretty certain.'

Daniel could not help sounding a little desperate. 'Well, they are wrong, completely wrong.'

Everett changed his point of attack. 'I know you have had some recent personal problems, Mr Felton, but have you been completely honest with us as to the reasons you are down here?'

Daniel remained silent for some seconds before nodding his head slowly.

Everett sounded a tad exasperated. 'I don't believe you are telling us the whole truth, Mr Felton. I suggest you give some serious thought to coming clean with us, because as it stands you are still a prime suspect for the murder of Duncan Fraser.' With that he rose abruptly from the sofa and moved towards the door.

Jack Wilkins just had time to give Daniel a comforting pat on the shoulder, before saying, 'Better give it some thought, Daniel, for your own good.'

After hearing the front door close, Daniel moved towards the window and watched the police car drive off in the pouring rain. He stood there motionless for a few minutes, before slumping back on the sofa with his head in his hands.

*

As the car joined the crawling queue behind a slow-moving farm vehicle, Martin Everett drummed his fingers on the steering wheel impatiently. Outside, the rain continued to patter down incessantly on the car roof in accompaniment to his rhythmic percussion. Ever since they had left Daniel Felton to drive back to Helston HQ, he had been uncharacteristically silent. Jack Wilkins suspected he had been quietly processing his thoughts on

Daniel. Everett suddenly gave a small cheer and moved smoothly through the gears, as the large tractor slowly trundled off the narrow road.

Wilkins felt it was a good opportunity to break the silence. 'What's your feeling about young Felton, sir?'

There was a brief reflective pause before he answered, 'Well, for a start, Jack, I don't appreciate being lied to. Putting that aside, my gut feeling is telling me that he is innocent of the Fraser murder, but he is definitely keeping something from us. Because of that and his pretty obvious mental fragility, I can't rule him out entirely.'

Wilkins had to agree. 'I must admit, for someone who's supposed to be innocent, he gets agitated very easily. What about the girl that says she saw him carrying the rucksack?'

'Despite the fact that PC Kent was not convinced by her, I think we will have to get back to her at some point. If she is lying, it's either a pathetic attempt to get her hands on the reward or there is something more suspicious going on. At the moment all leads are worth following up on.'

A thought occurred to Jack Wilkins. 'The cousin, Luke Sadler, seems a sensible sort. Do you think it might be a good idea to have another chat with him, voice our concerns regarding Daniel? It might throw some more light on the reasons for his cousin's mental state.'

Everett nodded. 'As I say, all avenues are worth pursuing.'

As they pulled up outside Helston HQ, Wilkins answered, 'We'll get on it straight away, sir.'

*

'OK, Mr Robinson, I'll go back to the seller and give him your verbal offer. Between you and me, I think he's going to want more, but I know for a fact that he is eager for a sale, so you never know. I'll get back to you.' Luke Sadler put the phone down and ticked off another client contact number. Considering it was the start of the working week, it had been a surprisingly busy day in his Hoxton office. A link in a chain of transactions had unexpectedly fallen through at the last moment, and he was doing his best to repair the damage. He glanced at his mobile phone for missed calls. There was one from a number he did not immediately recognise. After a quick check of his historic calls, he was slightly perturbed to see that it was from Sergeant Wilkins from the Cornish Constabulary.

He returned the call immediately. 'Hello, Sergeant Wilkins, sorry I missed your call.'

'Appreciate you calling back, Mr Sadler, can you spare a few minutes to talk?'

Luke stood up and moved to a quiet spot at the back of the office. 'Of course, there's nothing wrong, I hope?'

'I'm not sure, if I'm honest with you. The truth is we feel that your cousin is not doing himself any favours regarding the Fraser case.'

Luke was defensive. 'In what way exactly?'

'I won't beat about the bush, Mr Sadler, but it's pretty obvious to us that he is hiding something.'

Luke chose his next words carefully. 'I did tell you that he has been under a lot of strain lately. That's why he finds it difficult to handle anything remotely stressful at the moment.'

'I'm sorry to push you on this, Mr Sadler, but you will have to be more specific. There has been some new evidence come to light that links him with the Fraser murder.'

Luke felt his stomach lurch. 'What evidence?'

'Someone in the village has put him in the frame regarding the rucksack. It was recently recovered in a field, but I cannot say more than that at the moment.'

Luke's mind was reeling. Surely Daniel had not lost his head that night and got into a fight with the Scottish drifter? He refused to believe it. He then thought of the local hostility Daniel had been subjected to since his arrival at the cottage. There was more than a chance that this latest development had something to do with it. The beginnings of a plan began to formulate in his head. Momentarily lost in thought, he almost forgot that Sergeant Wilkins was waiting patiently on the end of the line for his response. 'The thing is, Sergeant Wilkins, I think someone in Tregarris is definitely out to cause Daniel some nasty mischief. I could tell you a bit more, but I would prefer to tell you face to face. I plan to come down in a day or so if that's OK?'

'The way the situation is with your cousin at the moment, I would say the sooner the better.'

'You have my word, Sergeant Wilkins.'

Luke looked pensive as he walked back to his desk. Despite his best efforts, Daniel's situation seemed to be getting more serious by the minute.

*

Mark Reid sat quietly in the lounge area of the Strathallan Guest House. He was savouring the warmth and flavour of his cappuccino. It was mid-afternoon and the atmosphere in the hotel felt sleepy and restful. He knew he had to make the phone call, but he was putting the moment off for as long as he could. The day before, he had waited around for Daniel Felton to leave the pub. He had then seen him make his way to the end of the high street and enter the Chough cottage. His detective intuition had proven correct and he had tracked down Daniel's whereabouts, but he had felt none of the usual satisfaction of a job well done. Instead he had been left feeling cheap and somehow diminished. Running into his old Met colleague had not helped. Seeing him, he had been reminded of a time when he had felt proud of what he did. A time when he had not been plagued by doubts that he was on the side of right. Should he really be helping dodgy characters like Joe Blades? More importantly, should he even be playing a part in making Daniel Felton's life more miserable? After all, he was just a kid. On the other hand, he had always prided himself on his professionalism, and he had taken this job in good faith. Quietly cursing Martin Everett for putting him in this moral dilemma, he reluctantly picked up his phone and searched for Joe Blades' number.

*

Luke finished off his last strand of spaghetti and sat back from the table fully sated. He silently congratulated himself. The meatballs had been just as he liked them – moist and spicy. Though the meal had been a joint effort after he and Kate had returned home from work, the meatballs had been his department. He felt he was getting better at this cooking lark. He allowed himself a celebratory sip of his Amarone wine. Not surprisingly, the dinner conversation had revolved around Sergeant Wilkins' phone call earlier that day and Luke's plans to return to Cornwall in the morning.

As usual, Kate was concerned for her friend. 'Lauren will be disappointed she cannot travel down there, what will you tell her?'

Luke looked serious. 'I will just have to tell her that something has to be sorted out first, but without going into too much detail.'

Kate had a sudden thought. 'Do you think there is a possibility that Daniel might have flipped that night and got into a fight with the drifter?'

Luke would not hear of it. 'I don't even want to think it. As I said, there are people in Tregarris who don't want him there.'

Kate reflected. 'If someone is really prepared to go that far to get Daniel into trouble, I suppose it's for the best that Lauren stays away.'

'Believe me, Kate, it definitely is. Who knows how far these people will go? They've definitely got a screw loose.'

Kate took his hand across the table. 'Promise me you'll be careful.'

'Don't worry. I'll be back before you know it.'

'Any idea how long you'll be there?'

'Hopefully it shouldn't be longer than a couple of days.'

'Don't forget the Audi is booked in for a service on Thursday.'

'That's why I'm taking the company car just in case.'

'Shall I invite Lauren to stay over again?'

Luke nodded. 'Good idea, be company for you and she'll probably need your support anyway.'

'She'll not be happy, that's for sure.'

Luke's thoughts turned to work. 'Are you OK picking up the reins with the broken property chain?'

Kate nodded reassuringly. 'I'm all over it, don't worry.'

Luke looked at her affectionately across the table. 'You are a true star. I suppose by way of thanks, I'm in charge of the washing-up.'

Kate smiled. 'There's no suppose about it.'

It was still dark when Luke left the house the following morning, his headlights piercing the gloom of the sleepy London streets. Stimulated by numerous gulps of freshly brewed black coffee, and with his Bluetooth connected for hands-free communication, he braced himself for the long drive ahead. He had been sorely tempted to give the name of Ricky Carlyon to Sergeant Wilkins, but he needed to be sure. Though he felt strongly that young Carlyon was involved somehow, he did not feel comfortable naming people to the police when he could not be certain. Fortunately there just might be a way to get some proof that his instincts were correct.

Over dinner the night before, he had not fully let on to Kate how concerned he was for his cousin. He felt anxious that he had not heard anything from Daniel after the accusation that he had some connection with the rucksack. He more than anyone knew his cousin's fragile mental state. The phone call with Lauren had not been easy, as she had already booked two days' holiday for that week. He had tried to strike the right balance, but she was no fool. She knew that it must be something serious. For all his good intentions, he was beginning to feel responsible for Daniel's predicament. He gave a heavy sigh and headed west through the City of London in the direction of the M4.

*

Mark Reid had finished his breakfast and was browsing the newspapers in the lounge of the Strathallan. It had been his intention to check out that morning and return to London to collect his payment from Joe Blades. But since he had made the phone call telling of Daniel's whereabouts, he had felt increasingly uncomfortable. There had been something in the way Joe Blades had said he could now leave the matter with him, that felt more than a touch sinister. Because of this feeling of unease, he had made the decision to stick around for a further few days. Besides, he had nothing to rush back to and he was enjoying the change of scene. He realised it would mean the occasional coastal trip into Tregarris, but that was no hardship. If that was what was needed to ease his conscience on Daniel, he was prepared to do it. He stretched out in the chair and ordered another coffee.

*

Luke Sadler gave the bell strap another pull. He could not help feeling a little anxious. He hoped that Daniel had not done anything silly. He had made good time in his journey down from London, but on his arrival at the cottage, it appeared to be empty, with Daniel nowhere to be seen. He saw that Daniel's car was still parked in front of the cottage, so hopefully he was not too far away. He peered through the lounge window but there was no sign of his cousin. It was early afternoon – surely the lazy bugger was still not in bed.

Luke took a key from his pocket and let himself in. Once inside the cottage it felt eerily empty. Entering the kitchen, Luke noticed there was an unwashed spoon and breakfast bowl left on the table. He shouted Daniel's name as he made his way up the stairs to the bedroom… there was no reply. Luke struggled to subdue his feelings of apprehension as he peered into the bedroom. He was relieved to see that it was unoccupied. Seeing that Daniel's bed was still unmade, it seemed like his cousin had not bothered with his domestic chores that morning. Luke thought that was a bad sign. He left the cottage and turned towards the coastal path. He thought it would be a good place to start looking for him, as he remembered Daniel saying how a good walk along the coastline often made him feel better.

Thankfully, Luke did not have to look too hard when he reached the path. In the distance he could just make out a solitary figure sitting down on a grass verge. As he drew nearer he was relieved to see it was Daniel looking dejectedly out to sea.

Luke did his best to sound cheerful. 'Penny for your thoughts?'

Daniel turned around with a look of surprise. 'What are you doing here?'

Luke sat down next to his cousin. He thought it best

to get straight to the point. 'Sergeant Wilkins rang me at work yesterday.'

Though he was pleased to see his cousin, Daniel sounded exasperated. 'Did he tell you that he thinks I'm a murderer?'

'Not exactly, but he did sound concerned.'

'I suppose he told you about the eyewitness?'

Luke nodded. 'Is there anything in it?'

Daniel's answer sounded a little desperate. 'I really don't need you to start doubting me as well. It's got to have something to do with Ricky Carlyon.'

'I don't suppose the police gave you a clue as to who it was that said they saw you?'

'Nothing at all, but from the way their big chief looked at me, I think he has already made up his mind. If only there was a way to find out if Carlyon's behind it.'

Luke looked thoughtful. 'There just might be.' He stood up and reached down for his cousin's hands. 'Come on, let's get back to the cottage, I could murder a cup of tea.'

Daniel reached up and allowed himself to be pulled to his feet. 'Have you said anything to Lauren?'

Luke thought back to that difficult conversation. He tried to lighten his tone. 'I told her that there were a couple of small issues to sort out before she came down here.'

Daniel looked concerned. 'I bet that didn't reassure her.'

Luke heard himself lie a little. 'She sounded OK with it.' He changed the subject. 'Here's the deal. If you get stuck into the housework when we get back, I will buy you a pint in the Pirate tonight. Does that sound good?'

Daniel smiled for the first time that day. 'You really are too good to me.'

Luke gave him a pat on the back. 'It's what cousins are for, I guess.'

On the short walk back to the cottage, Daniel felt his spirits lifting a little. Not for the first time, he wondered how he would cope without Luke.

*

Sandra Kent took a quick glance at the answer machine as she entered the hallway of her modern one-bedroom flat in Cambourne. As was usually the case, there was no light flashing. She thought that if it was not for her work, she might as well not bother to switch the thing on. She had been living in the flat for almost six months now, but she still didn't feel totally settled. The flat itself was cosy enough, but the long hours of her job had so far made it difficult for her to feel any emotional attachment. In a modern three-storey building on the outskirts of Cambourne, overlooking the River Cober, it was probably the nicest place she had ever lived in. The rent was pricey, but what else did she have to spend her money on? Also it was convenient, as it was only a twenty-minute drive along the B3303 into Helston. She sighed as she looked at the scattered clothing around her and the pile of washing in the basket. She was even letting the housework slip. Not that she was expecting company that night or even had a romantic date to look forward to. Her work saw to that. She'd tidy up her flat later, now all she wanted was a long, hot bath followed by an oven-ready lasagne and a glass of Merlot in front of the TV.

It was not long before she was wallowing in the hot scented water, with her thoughts turning to the Duncan Fraser case. They were going to pay a visit to Jenna Truscott in the morning. She felt that there was definitely something odd about that girl. Her account of her supposed sighting of Daniel Felton carrying the rucksack did not sound convincing somehow. It would be interesting to get Jack Wilkins' professional insight when they saw her tomorrow.

She thought once more of Daniel Felton. There would have been a time not so long ago that she would have gone for that type of boy. Good-looking but appealingly vulnerable. But not now; her fingers had been burned too many times. Now she increasingly found herself being drawn to men who offered stability and security. Maybe someone like Jack Wilkins? She chuckled inwardly at the thought. She allowed herself the thought of going out with him. In no way would you call him handsome, but he had a pleasant and kindly face. The slight age gap wouldn't be an issue, and she certainly enjoyed his company. He had a good sense of humour and could talk on a number of subjects. She had been told that it was a bad idea to get involved with people you work with, but where else was she likely to meet someone? It was a known fact that people who form relationships often meet at their places of work. Jack never talked much about his private life. She wondered if he was close to anyone. With that thought, she topped up her hot water, closed her eyes and drifted.

*

Luke Sadler crouched down low in the undergrowth and waited. Though it was dark, he had a good view of the clearing that overlooked the cottage. He had left the Jolly Pirate pub early, leaving Daniel to drink in the last orders with the two old men, Alf and Bill. If, as he suspected, it was young Carlyon who had been shouting the abuse, he was now in a great position to catch him red-handed. Earlier on in the pub, Luke had again noticed him giving them the evil eye. If he was responsible for the lies that were putting Daniel in the frame with the police, he was being very brazen about it. Either way, if his mum's disappointment about the cottage was behind all this, this would be a good opportunity to have it out with him.

The following fifteen minutes seemed to drag interminably, as he stooped there with only the sound of his breathing for company. Calculating that Daniel would be leaving the pub any time now, he straightened up a little to get a good view. It was then that he felt a sudden thud in his back. He felt himself stagger forward, before another blow to the side of his face knocked him to the ground. Momentarily stunned and shocked, he just managed to get a quick glimpse of a figure running away. It was dark and it had only been a glimpse, but he had seen enough to be sure of one thing. His attacker had not been Ricky Carlyon.

EIGHT

A THIEF AND A THUG

A lf and Bill were the last two customers to leave the bar, as Reg Turner, gently but firmly, ushered them towards the doors. 'Come on, you two, some of us want to get to bed tonight if you don't.' The two men grumbled a half-hearted protest but proceeded to shuffle slowly towards the exit. In the course of the evening, he had noticed them in the company of Daniel Felton.

'I hope you two have not been terrorising young Daniel again with your ghostly stories.'

Alf wagged a finger at him and replied, 'You might scoff, but we know what we know.'

Reg laughed. 'Filling his head with all that tosh, you'll give him nightmares.'

As the two men disappeared into the evening gloom, Reg heard Bill shout back, 'Forewarned is forearmed, that's all we're saying.'

Reg waved them away. 'Right on.'

Reg shook his head resignedly as he bolted the doors.

Old Tom would turn in his grave. Tom had never believed a word of the Black Dragon myth and he had lived in the Chough.

He went behind the bar and checked his till for the takings. Even though it was a Tuesday evening in early November, it still looked to be a good night's work. He made sure to go over the totals a couple of times, as he had noticed recently that the takings had fallen short of the correct amount. Not by much; a couple of quid here or a fiver there. Sure enough, the balance appeared to be out once again. At first he had thought that it might be down to his lazy arithmetic, but now it was beginning to look pretty obvious that someone was dipping their hands in the till. He thought there was no way it could be his bar staff. Betty and Annie occasionally worked in the bar on a casual basis. He had known them for years and he trusted them implicitly. He would have to keep his eyes open in future.

With the disconcerting knowledge that there could be a petty thief about the place, he turned out the lights and went upstairs.

*

'The bastard got the jump on me before I had a chance to react.' Luke Sadler was holding an icepack to the side of his face, as he sat in the kitchen of the Chough cottage.

Daniel was sitting opposite, with a look of anxious concern. 'And you're definitely sure it was not Carlyon?'

'One hundred per cent. He was bigger built and darker.'

Daniel thought back to the day he had seen Carlyon arguing with the other young man in the lane. From Luke's description, it could well have been the same person. He now recalled that there had been the distinct smell of burning in the lane that day. Had that been a pure coincidence? He did not know what to think. He ventured cautiously, 'I have seen Carlyon with another fella who kind of matches that description.'

'Do we know who he is?'

'No, I've only caught a glimpse of him a couple of times. I've never seen him drinking in the Pirate.'

Luke winced as he held the ice to his face. 'It's all too vague. We have to be surer than that.' He thought back to the unexpected assault. He still felt a little shaken and angry. 'If only I'd seen him coming,' he said bitterly.

Daniel felt responsible for his cousin's obvious discomfort. 'Are you sure you're alright?'

Luke waved a dismissive hand. 'Don't fuss. A couple of paracetamol and I'll be fine.'

Daniel looked distressed. 'This is entirely my fault – I should never have got you involved.'

Luke raised his voice. 'Don't talk rubbish. I came into this with my own free will.'

Daniel shouted back, 'Well, what are we going to do?'

Luke made a conscious effort to remain calm. 'My plan was to catch Carlyon red-handed before going to the police. Now it looks like it could be somebody else. As it stands you aren't doing yourself any favours by being secretive. I think it's about time we come clean with Sergeant Wilkins about the local harassment and the reasons you're down here.'

Daniel looked at the floor disconsolately. 'I thought the idea was for me to keep a low profile.'

Luke stood up and put a comforting hand on Daniel's shoulder. 'Things have changed, young fella, we have no choice. The last thing I want is the possibility of you getting charged with a murder you didn't commit.'

Despite feeling miserable Daniel managed a wry smile. 'I don't suppose profiles can get much higher than that.'

Luke chuckled through his throbbing jaw. 'Exactly, now where are those tablets?'

*

Jack Wilkins and Sandra Kent parked at the top of Fisherman's Lane and walked down the narrow thoroughfare to number 30. It had rained heavily in the night, but the puddles were now drying in the brisk autumnal breeze. Just on the outer fringes of Tregarris, it was an area that had somehow been left behind in the recent frenzied demand for holiday cottages and second homes. Most of the dwellings were occupied by a mix of the unemployed, teenage mothers and pensioners who couldn't afford to move. After Sandra Kent knocked firmly on the weather-beaten front door, they were greeted by the loud and incessant barking of a dog. There was some delay, before the door was opened by a short, dark-haired man who was more than a few pounds overweight. He was struggling to hold back a small, muscular terrier, which did not look to be the friendliest canine in Cornwall.

Jack Wilkins stood back a little. 'We would like to speak to Miss Truscott if she is around?'

The man seemed surprised. 'You want Jenna? What's she been up to?'

Sandra Kent answered, 'Nothing as far as we know. We just need to go over a statement she made last week. Is she in?'

The man gave a thin smile that somehow failed to reach his eyes. 'She's upstairs in bed. I'll see if I can get her up. I'll just put Scampi in the backroom.' The man pulled sharply on the collar of the terrier and disappeared to the rear of the house. He returned soon after and led them through a narrow vestibule that contained a rack for muddy shoes. Off to the side was a small living room which seemed even more cramped when they all filed in.

Wilkins wanted to know who he was dealing with. 'Are you Jenna's father?'

'Stepfather. Her real dad was drowned in a boating accident about six years back.'

'I'm sorry to hear that.'

'No need to be – take it from me, he was a real bastard.'

'Does Jenna's mum live here?'

The man looked a touch defensive. 'On and off.' He hesitated before continuing. 'At the moment it's off but she'll be back. She always calms down after a week or so.' He made his way up a narrow flight of stairs.

Sandra glanced at Wilkins and pulled a face. 'Not exactly a picture of domestic bliss, is it?'

Wilkins raised his eyebrows in acknowledgement.

They could just make out the voices coming from upstairs. The talking was hushed, but it sounded like there was plenty being said.

The man eventually returned looking a little flustered. 'She won't be a minute.'

There was an awkward two-minute silence before Jenna Truscott finally appeared on the stairs. She did not present an attractive picture. Her hair looked lifeless and badly cut, her nightdress shapeless and old-fashioned.

Sandra got straight to the point. 'Good morning, Jenna, we're sorry to get you out of bed. We just want to go over the statement you made last week if that's OK?'

Her heavy eyebrows seemed set in a permanent frown as she nodded to them.

'You are still sure that the man you saw carrying the rucksack was Daniel Felton?'

The girl seemed to hesitate for a moment, as if she was trying to make a calculation. 'I told you last week, didn't I?'

'And you still stand by what you said?'

She looked at the floor as she answered, 'Yes.'

Jack Wilkins had a question. 'How much of the rucksack did you see, Jenna? Most of it? Half of it?'

She took a long time to answer, as if she was having trouble remembering. 'About half of it with the straps.'

Sandra Kent turned her attention back to the man. 'Do you know where we can find Jenna's mum?'

'Not a clue to be honest. She's done it before. We have a row, she disappears for a couple of weeks, but she always comes back.'

'Can you give me her full name?'

'Diane Truscott, she sometimes goes by her maiden name, Smethwick.'

Wilkins wrote it down in his notebook. 'That'll do for now.'

Kent turned to Jenna and gave her a contact card with her number. 'Be sure to give us a call if you think of anything else, Jenna.'

The girl's face barely registered an expression as she nodded.

As they walked back to the car, Kent looked at Jack Wilkins. 'Well, what do you think?'

'She's lying through her teeth, there's no doubt about it. Which beggars the question, why?'

'It could be for the reward – they look like they could do with it.'

Wilkins agreed. 'True, but the family is a mess, there's no unity there. Could you see them all getting their heads together and coming up with a plan?'

'I know what you mean. They all sound like they hate each other. Which opens up the possibility that she could have hatched it up with someone outside the family.'

'As you said originally, the poor girl is definitely not the full ticket. She could easily have been put up to it.'

Sandra thought back to the girl's morose expression. 'It all seems rather sad. I'll see if we can track down the mother.'

As they drove away a message came over the radio from HQ. The desk sergeant informed them that Luke Sadler and Daniel Felton were at the station in Helston and wanted to talk to them.

Kent whistled through her teeth. 'Surely it can't be a confession from Daniel after all this time?'

Jack Wilkins remembered his recent telephone conversation with Luke Sadler and shook his head. 'When I spoke to the cousin on Monday, he hinted there could be some new information in the pipeline – it's probably that.'

He pointed the car in the direction of Helston and put his foot down.

Some twenty minutes after Wilkins and Kent had departed Fisherman's Lane, Jenna Truscott left her house and took a bus for the short ride inland to the once-thriving tin-mining village of Bosnick. Reaching the outskirts of the village, Jenna gazed abstractedly out of the window. Though the mining industry in that area had long since ceased, a few of the distinctive, disused structures still remained standing. With their white chimneys pointing defiantly towards the grey sky, they gave the open landscape an added desolate air. Not that Jenna would have noticed... her mind was far too preoccupied with other matters. She was on her way to see him. She had done what he had asked. Now she longed for him to fulfil his promise and be her boyfriend.

The bus came to a halt in a street with a row of identical-looking houses. Built back in the day when the tin mines were thriving, the small mining houses had provided the workers and their families with much-needed shelter and accommodation. Jenna approached the house at the far end of the row, knocked on the door and waited.

*

'You look like you have been in the wars,' observed Jack Wilkins, as he took a seat opposite Luke Sadler and Daniel Felton. Wilkins was referring to the bluish-coloured swelling on the side of Luke Sadler's jaw.

Luke put a hand to his face self-consciously. 'You could say that.'

Sandra Kent returned from the vending machine with a tray of teas. 'Help yourselves; sorry it's not a brew from the pot.' She sat down alongside Jack Wilkins.

Wilkins opened a small notebook. 'Now, what have you got to tell us?'

The two cousins glanced at each other briefly, before Luke took the responsibility to begin the dialogue. 'I think a good place to start is by telling you exactly how Daniel came to be down here.'

Wilkins could not help sounding a touch sardonic. 'I think it's about time, don't you?'

Luke gave a rueful grin. 'It is true that Daniel came down from London because of personal problems. But you are correct to suspect that he has not been totally open with you.'

Wilkins sat up a little. 'Go on.'

'Over the last year Daniel somehow developed a gambling addiction that got totally out of control. When I finally got to find out the extent of the problem, he had already mounted some considerable debts. It had not taken too long for some unsavoury people to get wind and the loan sharks soon started circling. When Daniel finally called me he was already at rock bottom: he had given up his job and was pretty close to splitting up with his long-term girlfriend. He had already been physically threatened, so I thought the best thing was to get him away from London. I had already purchased the cottage in Tregarris; it seemed the obvious place to keep a low profile and give him some breathing space.'

Sandra looked across at Daniel. 'Have you managed to stop gambling?'

Daniel found his voice. 'That's the good news since I have been down here: I haven't even thought of it. It's as if I left that world behind me in London.'

Luke went on. 'Obviously the last thing Daniel needed was a body to be found on his doorstep, with all the fuss and publicity that goes with it.'

Jack Wilkins leaned forward. 'So why are you telling us now?'

'Simple, when you told me that someone was now putting Daniel in the frame for the murder, I thought the time had come to hold nothing back.'

Both Kent and Wilkins nodded encouragement but said nothing.

Daniel took his cue. 'The fact is, since I arrived in Tregarris I have been the victim of some low-level harassment almost from day one.'

It was Sandra Kent that asked the obvious question. 'Can you give us some examples?'

Daniel's face clouded as he remembered. 'Hostile looks, shouted abuse, doorbell-ringing in the early hours, car vandalism.'

Jack Wilkins interrupted sharply, 'So are you telling me that the damage to the Fiat did take place outside the cottage on the night of the murder?'

Daniel looked both stressed and ashamed as he answered, 'Yes.'

Wilkins shook his head. 'You really should have told us at the time, Daniel – as it is you've done yourself no favours.'

Daniel looked down at the table. 'I know.'

Sandra looked at Luke. 'So, how did you get the sore jaw?'

Luke was reminded once more of the throbbing sensation in his face. 'I was coming to that.' He composed himself before continuing. 'Daniel had been verbally abused on several occasions on his way home from the Jolly Pirate. It was always in the evening and the shouts came from somewhere high above. I did a bit of a recce and discovered a narrow path that passed behind the pub. It wound up the hill and led to a small clearing that looked down on the cottage. It seemed obvious it was the place where the abuser had been standing.'

Wilkins interjected, 'I think I'm beginning to see where this is going.'

Luke went on. 'Well, last night, I decided to take a look up there while Daniel left the pub, see if I could get to the bottom of it. Unfortunately the bugger got the jump on me and gave me a clout.'

'Did you manage to get a look at him?' Kent asked.

Luke touched his jaw gingerly. 'Only a glimpse unfortunately.'

'Do you think you would recognise him if you saw him again?'

Luke thought back to the burly figure he saw retreating into the darkness. 'Not with any certainty. He was a big guy; he ran up the hill away from the village.' He suddenly remembered the cigarette butts. 'I think he could well be a smoker.'

Both Kent and Wilkins sat up. 'What makes you say that?' Wilkins asked.

'The amount of cigarette butts I found on the ground above the cottage.'

'You say the lane wound up behind the Jolly Pirate?'

'Yes.'

Wilkins made a mental note to pay it a visit as soon as possible. He turned to Daniel. 'You say you were threatened back in London?'

Daniel thought back to the two men. 'Yes, two big guys smartly dressed in suits.'

'Do you have any idea who they were working for?'

Daniel thought of the well-dressed man in the pub. 'The only person I can think of was this guy who approached me in my local. We got talking and he was soon offering to lend me some money. Looking back, it was obviously no accidental meeting. I was a complete fool.'

'Can you describe him?'

'He would have been in his mid-thirties, very dapper. I think he wore a wrist bracelet.'

'How much do you owe him?'

'Nowhere near what they're asking, that's for sure.'

Luke added, 'We've paid the bulk of the other debts, but I refuse to pay anything to those sharks.'

Wilkins reassured him on that point. 'You're right not to do so.' He wrote down the descriptions. 'OK, we'll get our friends in Scotland Yard to make some enquiries.'

He turned back to Daniel. 'I take it you're not thinking of returning to London anytime soon?'

There was no hesitation from Daniel. 'No chance.'

'Good.' Wilkins sat back in his chair and studied the faces of the two young men in front of him. 'Can you think of anything else to add?'

Luke was in two minds, but he decided to mention Ricky Carlyon. 'Though it wasn't the dude who thumped me last night, there's a regular who drinks in the Jolly Pirate that's openly hostile and we know he's not happy that I purchased the Chough cottage. Seems his mum had designs on it and was pretty upset when she was priced out.'

'Who told you this?'

'The pub landlord Reg. He told us in confidence.'

'Do you have this person's name?'

It was Daniel that finally answered, 'Ricky Carlyon.'

*

Jenna Truscott was having trouble fighting back the tears as she boarded the bus that took her back to Tregarris from Bosnick. But they were not just the tears of rejection; they were also tears of anger and betrayal. She had done what he had asked. She had told the police what he had wanted. It had been his turn to deliver on his promise to be her boyfriend. Instead he had laughed in her face as if it had been one big joke all along. He had even continued to call her by that horrible name that he said suited her so well... Pug! On the short journey home she sat at the back of the bus, heartbroken and alone with her dark, festering thoughts.

*

Reg Turner had just called last orders for the afternoon, when Jed Harris came out of the kitchens and beckoned him over. Jed had been his pub chef for the best part of three years now and had a growing reputation. Reg wondered how much longer he would have his services. Good chefs were hard to find and even harder to hold on to.

'Problem, Jed?'

'Hope not. I need to have a half day on Monday next week if that's OK; got an open day at the school and young Melanie wants me to be there.'

Reg had a soft spot for Jed's daughter Melanie because of her affection for Rusty. There had been the odd occasion when she had taken him out for a walk when he had been too busy. 'No bother, Jed, I hardly think we'll be snowed under on Monday.'

'Thanks, Reg. I've had a word with Tony and he's OK with it.'

Reg laughed. 'He's got no choice.' Tony was the keen young apprentice chef who still had a way to go to match Jed's culinary skills. 'Will he be up to it?'

'He's getting there – only another ten years, I reckon,' Jed joked sarcastically.

Reg pulled a face. 'I reckon I'll be long gone by then.' He had a thought. 'How's the new kitchen porter getting on?' Reg was talking about George Rosie, a young man he had employed on a month's trial.

Jed frowned. 'I'm not impressed, to be honest. He's well capable and he can be charming enough when the mood's upon him, but there are times when his mind seems to be somewhere else. Did you know he writes poetry?'

Reg looked surprised. 'First I've heard of it.'

Jed went on. 'Looking at his expression sometimes, I wouldn't even like to hazard a guess what's going on in his head. It doesn't help that he keeps disappearing outside for a fag every ten minutes.'

Reg was disappointed with what he was hearing. 'I don't like the sound of that. I'd taken him on in good faith. Looks like I will have to have a word with him.'

Jed agreed. 'It's a shame because I think there's a good worker in there somewhere.'

Reg cleared some empty glasses from the bar. 'Leave it with me.'

*

Sometime after Luke and Daniel had left the police station, Jack Wilkins and Sandra Kent were sitting at their desks taking a fresh look at the Fraser case, armed with the new information the cousins had given them.

Kent was looking at her screen when she suddenly gave a small cry of recognition. 'Jenna Truscott's mum is known to us under her maiden name, Smethwick. Got a few recent charges against her for drunken affray and causing a disturbance. For a mum approaching middle age she looks like she gets about a bit. A few of these incidents took place in Newquay, one in Plymouth and one in St Ives.'

Wilkins looked up from his screen. 'Doesn't sound

like poor Jenna has had much luck in life.'

Kent thought back to their visit to the house that morning. It seemed that some people were fated to be dealt a bad hand right from the moment they were born; Jenna seemed to be one of those people.

Martin Everett entered the room. He'd had to attend another meeting for the big chiefs at Exeter HQ that morning. He'd got to the stage in his career when meetings increasingly seemed an unnecessary interruption to the everyday routine; especially when it involved a round trip of two hundred miles.

He was eager to catch up with events. 'Any further forward on the Fraser case?'

Jack Wilkins brought him up to speed with the visit to the station by the cousins. He then handed him the official note sheet from the interview.

Everett studied it with interest. 'So he was on the run from loan sharks – I knew he was keeping something back.'

Wilkins nodded. 'It looks like the threat of a murder charge forced them to reveal all.'

'They've been silly boys. We should have had that information from the start.'

'Tomorrow morning we're going into Tregarris first light. We'll take a look at this lane behind the pub and pick up a sample of the cigarette butts.'

Everett was looking intrigued. 'If the boys are telling the truth, this case is getting more interesting by the minute. I think it's a good bet that any DNA found on the butts matches that found at the murder scene.'

'It would tie in neatly if they do.'

Everett continued reading the notes. 'Mr Sadler was quite definite that this Ricky Carlyon was not the man that clumped him?'

Wilkins confirmed. 'He was positive about that. Just the same, I've looked up Carlyon's address on the electoral role. He lives just off the high street in Tregarris, so we thought it might be a good idea to drop in and pay him a visit while we're there tomorrow.'

Everett nodded his approval. 'It's definitely worth a dig. I'll take care of the London end. I still have some useful contacts in the Yard.' As he gave the sheet back to Jack Wilkins he looked quite exhilarated. 'I feel the net is closing in.'

*

Luke was just entering the outskirts of London. He had made good time on his journey back from Cornwall. He really hoped that the decision to reveal all at Helston Police Station would lead to a positive change in Daniel's fortunes. He had felt a touch reluctant when he had left Daniel back at the cottage, but he needed to get back to Kate and his property business. He'd go back over the weekend – perhaps all this business with Duncan Fraser would be sorted by then and Kate and Lauren could come with him. He was not looking forward to explaining the large bruising on his jaw to Kate.

He glanced at the time; it was just after six-thirty, so Kate would probably be at home by now. He called her up. It was good to hear her voice.

'Hi, Luke.'

'Hi, hun, it looks like I'll be with you in about thirty minutes.'

'Great, I'll get in a takeaway. Chinese or Indian?'

'Not fussed, I'll let you choose. How's business?'

'Still buzzing, Mr Hanson rang about twenty times as usual. He cannot seem to get it in his head that people need time to make decisions.'

Luke laughed. 'He's a serial worrier, that one. He wants everything to be tied up in a week.'

'Then it's about time he got real. Do I dare ask how Daniel is?'

'He's OK in the circumstances. I've got plenty to tell you, nothing serious but not all of it good.'

'Now you've got me worried.'

Luke reassured her, 'No need to be, hun.' He quickly changed the subject. 'How was Lauren?'

'She knows something is going on – you didn't do a good job convincing her there was nothing to worry about.'

Luke thought back to the awkward phone call. 'I must admit, it wasn't an easy conversation.'

'She's not silly. When is Daniel going to tell her?'

'I think he's going to give her a call tomorrow.'

'Good, it's best to be open with her. I'd better get these takeaways ordered. See you in a bit, hun.'

As Luke turned the car towards East London he caught sight of his reflection in the rear mirror. The bruising on his swollen jaw was still quite prominent. Suddenly the thought of arriving home and seeing Kate did not seem quite so attractive.

*

Reg Turner woke up with a slight start. He sat up in bed, his heart beating fast. Some sound in the night had disturbed him. He stared into the darkness and listened. There was a faint sound of something coming from the bar area downstairs. His first thought was that Rusty had somehow got into the pub from his kennel in the backyard. He got up and put on his dressing gown, before gently opening the bedroom door. He made his way along the landing and slowly descended the stairs. It was then that he noticed the backdoor was swinging wide open – a chill early November breeze sending a cold shiver up his spine. The bolt on the door had been playing up recently and he had meant to get it fixed. He looked out into the murky, shadowy backyard; as far as his eyes could make out there was no one there. He pulled the door shut and turned on the downstairs light. He hoped that the noises he had heard had been caused by the breeze from the open door. All the same, he could not help calling out, 'Anybody there?' as he entered the bar area. His shout was met with silence as his eyes scanned around the bar. Thankfully the large room appeared to be devoid of any intruder. He was just about to return to his bedroom, when he noticed the till behind the bar was open. He saw almost immediately that it had been emptied. It was at that moment that he heard Rusty barking from outside. He rushed to the backdoor, which was again wide open. He looked out. There was nothing to be seen, but he did hear a car driving away. It appeared the thief had bolted and vanished into the night.

NINE

TRAGEDY STRIKES

Jack Wilkins and Sandra Kent stood looking down on Chough cottage from the top of the lane that ran up from behind the Jolly Pirate. If Daniel Felton was telling them the truth, then they had to concede that the abuser could not have chosen a better vantage point to do the deed. They looked out above the cottage towards the sea. Though the morning was overcast and breezy, with threatening dark clouds looming on the Atlantic horizon, the view was still stunningly impressive.

Kent was holding a plastic forensic bag with some sample cigarette butts which she had collected from the ground. She looked further up the hill. 'Luke Sadler said that his attacker ran off in that direction... I wonder where it leads to?'

Wilkins started walking up the hill. 'There's only one way to find out.'

The lane wound upwards for a further fifty metres before coming to a halt on a small minor road that served as one of the numerous thoroughfares into Tregarris. About fifteen yards along the road there was a narrow layby which could just about have accommodated a small car.

Kent remarked, 'Handy for a quick getaway from the village if needed.'

Wilkins nodded in agreement but said nothing.

They slowly made their way back down the lane towards the high street. After placing the forensic bag in the boot of the police car, they walked the short distance to Number 6 Pendale Close: the home of Ricky Carlyon. The tiny structure was a typical end-of-terrace cottage made of Cornish granite that dated back a hundred years or more. They knocked on a front door that looked like it could do with a fresh lick of paint. It was promptly answered by a bright-eyed woman, aged somewhere in her mid-fifties.

She saw the two uniforms and immediately jumped to the wrong conclusion. 'I've already been asked about the dead man on the coastal path, I told the officer all I knew about him.'

Sandra Kent smiled politely and cut in quick, 'We appreciate any help you may have given us so far in our enquiries, but we do have some further questions.' Having previously confirmed on the electoral role that Ricky Carlyon lived with his mum, Kent went on, 'I take it you are Mrs Elsie Carlyon… Ricky's mum?'

There was an immediate look of concern on her face. 'Is this about Ricky? What has he been up to?'

'Would it be possible for us to come in for a few minutes and discuss it inside?'

Still wearing a worried face, she ushered them into a small living area where the furniture was solid and serviceable. Sandra thought it felt cosy.

After sitting down opposite each other, Jack Wilkins got down to business. 'Is Ricky upstairs?'

'No, he's just popped out to get me a loaf of bread. What's this about?'

'I understand that you wanted to move from here to the Chough cottage.'

Elsie looked surprised. 'How did you get to hear about that?'

'Is it correct?'

'After Ricky's dad cleared off, Old Tom, who lived in the Chough, became a good friend of mine. I always loved the cottage and Tom said that he liked the thought that one day I might have it after he was gone. It broke my heart when Tom died and I didn't get it. But what's that got to do with Ricky?'

Kent answered, 'It seems that someone has been giving the person who is staying there a hard time.'

Realisation dawned on Elsie Carlyon's face. 'And you think it's my Ricky?'

'We have reason to think he might be involved.'

They were interrupted by the front door opening as Ricky Carlyon returned with the loaf of bread. He looked unnerved by the sight of the uniformed police. 'Wha… what's going on?'

His mum beckoned him over to sit next to her on the couch. 'It seems that someone has been causing problems for the people in the Chough. I hope you haven't been doing anything silly, Ricky?'

Wilkins noticed that the young man seemed to take strength from the close proximity of his mum and had regained his composure. 'Of course I haven't.'

Wilkins looked him in the eye. 'Is it true that you were deeply upset when your mum failed to purchase the Chough?'

He looked disgruntled as he answered, 'Wouldn't you be? My mum had set her heart on it. All these Emmets buying second homes is pricing us out of the market.'

Elsie Carlyon joined in. 'It's a killer for the youngsters – how are they supposed to get on the ladder today?'

Ricky went on. 'A lot of my mates have had to move away.'

Wilkins could see that Ricky was bitter and a bit of a mummy's boy. But did that make him the abuser on the hill? After all, Luke Sadler had been pretty certain it was someone else who had clobbered him. Besides which, he guessed there were probably many others in Tregarris that felt as he did.

Meanwhile Elsie Carlyon was warming to the subject. 'People say that the tourism is booming, but at what cost? Friends are moving away, families are drifting apart and customs are dying out. We've lost the community.'

Sandra Kent had some sympathy for their sentiments, but she was there to do a job. She turned her attention back to Ricky. There were no obvious signs he was a smoker. She studied his features closely once more. He would not have been bad-looking if it wasn't for the almost permanent scowl that soured his expression. 'So you can honestly say that you have had nothing to do with the harassment?'

'No.'

Did his eyes waver for just a moment before his one-word answer? Sandra thought it was difficult to tell. 'Are you a regular customer in the Jolly Pirate, Ricky?'

'Of course I am. It's one of the few places to go around here.'

Wilkins turned back to Elsie. 'Do you mind me asking how long it's been since your husband left, Mrs Carlyon?'

'Ten very long years – it's never easy bringing up a young boy on your own.' She gave Ricky a hug. 'I've always wanted Ricky to have a normal life. It's hard to know how much discipline to apply. He may not have had many material things, but I've always tried to give him plenty of love.'

Wilkins and Kent were left with plenty to think about when they eventually left the Carlyons' house and walked back to the car.

Kent spoke first. 'The mum seemed decent enough, but I can't make up my mind about Ricky.'

Wilkins agreed, 'I know what you mean. He's not totally convincing and he's definitely not happy.'

They were just about to return to Helston, when a call came in from HQ informing them about the burglary in the Jolly Pirate from the night before.

Jack Wilkins turned to Kent with a wry grin. 'It all seems to be happening in Tregarris.'

Ten minutes later they were standing at the backdoor of the Jolly Pirate with Reg Turner.

Jack Wilkins was examining the faulty bolt with interest. 'You say it's recently been playing up?'

Reg confirmed, 'The last couple of weeks it's been

temperamental. I was meaning to get it fixed. Looks like I left it too late.'

'I may be mistaken, but it's possible that someone had previously loosened it with a chisel. See that groove in the woodwork?'

Reg leaned forward to take a closer look. 'I'll be jiggered, so it is.'

Wilkins noticed that the gents' toilet was only a few yards away. He nodded towards it. 'Looks like any number of people would have had the opportunity. Did anyone else know that the bolt was loose?'

Reg thought hard. 'Not as far as I know, though I suppose anyone could have noticed it.'

'We'll get forensics over to take a look. Maybe the intruder left some dabs, though somehow I doubt it. It has all the hallmarks of it being planned.'

They walked through to the bar area and examined the till. 'How much did you say was missing?'

Reg pulled a pained expression. 'As I say, I've recently noticed some small amounts going missing, but last night it was about £300. I'm well pissed off because most evenings I empty the till after closing. I was a bit tired last night and it just went out of my mind. It wouldn't be the first time I've done that, but up till now there had never been a problem. Needless to say, I won't be doing it again.'

Wilkins looked sympathetic. 'Unfortunately you only have to be unlucky once. The one night you don't do it, it's always the way. What you can do is make sure you get that lock repaired as soon as possible.'

Reg shook his head ruefully. 'I suppose I'd better get

the doors open for the lunchtime rush, see if I can get some of my money back.'

'Good idea.'

As they left the pub to return to the car, Jack Wilkins recognised Martin Everett's old colleague from the Met walking along the high street. What was his name... Reid? What was he doing here in Tregarris? He would have to remember to mention it to his boss. After briefly mentioning the sighting to Sandra, they drove out of Tregarris, with both of them feeling they had more questions than answers. If they had taken one more glance behind them, they would have seen Mark Reid entering the Jolly Pirate as one of Reg Turner's first customers of the day.

*

Daniel stood in the churchyard with his phone to his ear. He was talking to Lauren. She sounded stressed. 'It must be something serious for Luke to stop me coming down to see you.'

Daniel did his best to reassure her. 'We just have to sort out a couple of issues, that's all.'

Lauren's patience finally snapped, as she shouted, 'Will you please tell me what's going on?'

Daniel's voice faltered slightly. 'A man was found dead on the coastal path and someone has mistakenly put me in the frame.' There was a deathly quiet at the end of the line. Daniel felt his voice becoming increasingly desperate. 'The thing is, I don't think the police are totally sure of my innocence so I still have to convince them.' The silence at the other end of the line was deafening. Daniel pleaded, 'You do believe me, don't you?'

There was a slight sob in Lauren's voice when she finally answered, 'I need to think. I honestly don't know what to believe anymore.' The line went dead.

Feeling totally despondent, Daniel put the phone back in his pocket and slowly made his way back to the village.

Stepping out of the shadows, the man they called Vince watched him go.

*

Mark Reid sat in the bar of the Jolly Pirate savouring the last few dregs of his pint. Unfortunately his Cornish excursion was coming to an end. He had extended his stay for as long as he could, but it was time for him to get back to London and claim his fee from Joe Blades. He also had the small matter of removing the GPS tracker from Luke Sadler's car. It was a shame he had to go back; he felt so relaxed. He could not remember the last time he had felt so much in the moment. Looking back over his life it seemed to have been one long road of marriage, career, mortgage, promotion boards, financial struggles, divorce and pensions. These last few days in Cornwall had brought home to him that there could be a more enjoyable way to exist. Another way to enjoy the life he had remaining. His one outstanding disquiet was the welfare of Daniel Felton. He made the decision that before he left for home, he would ring his old colleague Martin Everett and voice his concerns. He could then leave with a clear conscience and hopefully Daniel would be in safe hands.

With his mind settled on the matter of Daniel, it was coincidental that he should catch sight of him as he exited the Jolly Pirate. He could see immediately that Daniel looked distracted and upset. He followed at a distance as he watched him head towards the Chough. Much to his surprise, Daniel walked straight past the cottage and went on in the direction of the coastal path. The weather conditions did not look ideal for a walk along the coast. It was starting to rain heavily and a discernible mist was beginning to descend from the afternoon sky.

Reid was just about to turn around and head back to the high street, when a man suddenly appeared from the direction of the Chough. From his stealthy body language, it was obvious he was stalking Daniel as he walked towards the path. There was something familiar about the figure: his large athletic build, the way he moved. Reid felt a surge of adrenaline as recognition finally dawned. It was Max Roberts, a well-known London heavy. Unfortunately it appeared that the fears he had felt for Daniel's welfare had proved well founded. It looked pretty obvious that Max had been employed by Joe Blades to dish out some well-targeted intimidation and fear. He knew from experience that Roberts was chillingly good at that: it came natural to him. This was getting serious. He hurriedly fished in his pocket for DI Everett's card. He rang the number.

*

Luke Sadler was sat in his office in Hoxton looking troubled. He had just received a call from the garage where his Audi was being serviced. They had just given him the disturbing news that they had found a tracking device in his wheel arch. Sitting there struggling to make sense of it, he suddenly recalled Kate mentioning she had recently noticed an occupied Ford Fiesta parked outside the office on more than one occasion. At the time he had not given it much thought. But now he was pretty convinced that it must have had something to do with Daniel. Though he had not driven directly to Tregarris in the Audi, he had used the car previously for his trip to Helston. Feeling a rising concern, he decided to give Sergeant Wilkins a call. Helston HQ took a while to pick up before answering.

'Can you put me through to Sergeant Wilkins, please?'

'Hold on.' There was a further minute of silence before the operator replied, 'Sorry, he is not available at the minute, he has been called out to an urgent incident. I would suggest you call back later.'

Luke was not listening to the last part. His blood had run cold.

*

Daniel felt his tears mingling with the driving rain as he wandered aimlessly along the coastal path. The phone call with Lauren had left him feeling utterly distraught. She had made it pretty obvious from her emotional reaction that even she now doubted him. Lost in the misery of his thoughts, he barely noticed the figure in the distance walking towards him. It was only as he drew near that he noticed it was a man. Daniel felt his stomach lurch as he immediately recognised the man's menacing sneer. It was one of the men who had threatened him back in London.

He went to turn back the way he had come, but his escape route was cut off. The other heavy who had partnered him in London was blocking the way. Daniel felt sick with fear.

The man before him continued to smirk maliciously, before shouting above the wind and rain, 'Fancy seeing you here, Mr Felton. It's a small world, I guess.'

Daniel remained silent. He could think of nothing to say.

The man laughed. 'Cat got your tongue, Mr Felton?'

The other man behind Daniel stood silent and unsmiling, his body language somehow nonchalantly sinister.

The first man suddenly advanced swiftly towards Daniel and grabbed the collar of his parka. His face was uncomfortably close. 'I don't want to have to hurt you, Daniel, but we do still have the small matter of your debts to settle. I take it you were planning to return to London after this little holiday?'

Daniel just about managed a slight nod of the head.

'As you can imagine, our man in London is not best pleased with you running away. Especially after you promised him you would pay all the money you owe. As it is, it looks like I may have to let Max loose on you.'

Daniel heard a deep chuckle from the man behind him. He turned around and squinted desperately through the rain at the malevolent expression on the man's face. Struggling to stifle a despairing sob, he steeled himself for the worst.

It was then that they heard a voice, struggling to compete with the howling wind. 'I hope you are not going to do anything silly, boys.' It was Mark Reid. He had managed to creep up on them and was now standing behind the silent man he knew as Max Roberts. It had not surprised him to see that Max had an accomplice, even less so that it was Vince Mitchell. He knew from past experience that the two men had worked together a long time in the business of intimidation.

Mitchell let go of Daniel's collar in surprise. 'What's it to do with you?'

Reid shouted back, 'I really don't like to see someone being bullied. It's as simple as that.'

Vince squinted through the driving rain. He had the vague feeling he had seen the man before but couldn't place him. 'Is that so? I think you would be wise to carry on walking and mind your own business.'

'I'm sorry. I really can't do that.'

Mark Reid was playing for time. The police should be arriving any minute. What was keeping them? He suddenly felt a vice like grip on his shoulders, followed by Max's menacing voice in his ear. 'Oh, I think you can.' The big man had got the jump on him.

Though caught by surprise, Reid saw an opportunity. Seeing that Daniel was momentarily free to run away, he shouted, 'Run, Daniel!' before turning and twisting in Max's grip.

Daniel needed no further instruction; in an instant he was away from Vince's clutching hands and running back towards the village for all his worth.

Though Max Roberts was a big unit, Reid forcefully used his body weight to pull him off balance. As the momentum forced them both backwards, Mark Reid felt his foot give way underneath him. For five precarious seconds the two of them spun in a perilous pirouette, before they both over-balanced and disappeared over the edge of the coastal path. The two men were to remain locked in an eternal embrace as they hurtled to the rocks below.

For some seconds, Vince Mitchell stood transfixed in shock. The horror had all unfolded in front of him so quickly, yet the mental flashback he'd just witnessed seemed to keep playing back to him in slow motion. He eventually moved cautiously to the edge of the path and looked over. The two men were lying quite still on a solitary boulder, caressed by the lapping waves and still gruesomely locked together in a mass of twisted limbs. Vince stood there mesmerised by the sight, a sick feeling bubbling in the pit of his stomach.

He was brought back urgently into the moment by somebody shouting. It was Sergeant Wilkins, accompanied by two uniformed officers. On seeing the uniform, Vince's immediate instinct was to run away. He made a dash for the lane that led back across the fields towards the village.

After closing the gate behind her and entering the field, it did not take long for Sandra Kent to see the man running frantically towards her. Though he was still some distance away, the man's athletic build more than matched the description she had been given. She had been delegated to take the back path through the churchyard in order to cut off any such escape route. Her pulse quickened as she took cover in the hedge that framed the field. She remembered that Jack Wilkins' last words had been to remind her that the two men were known to be dangerous, so she had to be sensible in calculating any risk. Crouched in the hedge, she could feel her own breathing becoming more rapid as she heard the man's heavy footfall drawing closer. She steeled herself and waited for the right moment.

Vince had only managed to get halfway across the field before Sandra Kent appeared from nowhere and pounced on his back. He swore and flung his elbows back savagely, but Sandra continued to hang on tenaciously. She let out a cry as a flailing elbow hit her squarely in the eye, but she continued to cling on with grim determination. As Vince contorted his body in every direction in an attempt to throw her off his back, she could feel her grip gradually loosening. With the strength beginning to drain from her, she began to slide slowly but surely towards the ground.

It was at that point that she heard the welcome voice of Jack Wilkins. 'Great work, Sandra, I reckon we can take it from here.'

*

Daniel felt his legs beginning to buckle with exhaustion as he finally came to a halt. He had no idea for how long or how far he had run; he only knew that he needed to get as much distance as he possibly could between him and the two men. As he stood there in the wind and rain, trembling and drained of energy, a wave of morbid despair crept over him. Not for the first time, he felt he was losing his sanity. Feeling nauseous and dizzy, he sat down on the grass verge that skirted the path. His original instinct had been to run back towards the cottage, but on seeing the police cars approaching he had continued running along the path. What did they want? Were they coming to arrest him for the murder of Duncan Fraser? Why did no one believe him? Now even Lauren doubted him. He felt that his life had descended into one long nightmare in which there could only be one ending. He got up unsteadily and looked down onto the jagged rocks below. He moved closer to the edge. Just one small step and all his misery could be over. It would be so easy…

*

It had been a busy afternoon at Helston HQ. The Cornwall Search and Rescue Team had taken some time in retrieving the bodies of Max Roberts and Mark Reid in the difficult weather conditions. It had caused a significant delay in the resultant paperwork and numerous written reports that were a necessary requirement after such a tragic incident. It was one of those situations when staff numbers suddenly felt a bit stretched. This had not been helped by the fact that Sergeant Wilkins had accompanied PC Kent to the Helston Community Hospital to get her eye checked out.

DI Everett looked thoughtfully across the desk at Vince Mitchell, as the big man finished his account of the events that had led to the tragic death of Mark Reid. From what Mitchell had told him, it sounded like Reid had died a hero's death. Everett now felt he owed it to his old mentor to get the man behind the money-lending operation. In the brief and urgent phone call he had received from Reid earlier, he'd mentioned the two heavies were working for someone in London. Unfortunately any hopes of Reid revealing who that could have been had been killed off with his old Met colleague's demise. Since returning to Helston HQ, Martin Everett had deliberately left the traumatised Vince Mitchell to stew in the cells for a bit: now he was going to turn the screw. There was no doubt Mitchell was a nasty piece of work, but he was after the organ grinder not the monkey. Men like Mitchell and the now-dead Max Roberts were minnows in the bigger scheme of things. He was after the bigger fish. After some further deliberation he finally made his move.

He placed a pad and pencil in front of the big man. 'Here's what we're going to do, Vince. You give me the name of the man you are working for in London, and I will let you walk away from this mess a free man.'

Mitchell looked back at him with a cold stare and remained silent.

Everett was undaunted, as he nodded once more towards the pad and pencil. 'You have my word on it. Relocation, new identity, it's your choice.'

Mitchell was still in a state of deep shock. He felt numb. With Max gone for good, nothing was ever going to be the same again. The option that the copper was presenting looked like his only opportunity to start afresh and take a different route. In the criminal world there were always risks involved in disloyalty, but he was prepared to take that chance. In that moment it really did not seem a difficult decision. He slowly reached across for the pencil.

*

As soon as Sandra Kent managed to satisfy the doctor that there was no permanent damage to her badly bruised eye, all she wanted was to get back to her Cambourne flat, have a shower and get a good night's sleep. She agreed to Jack Wilkins' suggestion to drive her home, as she was in no fit condition to drive herself. The painful encounter with Vince Mitchell had shaken her more than she cared to admit. She had already taken some paracetamol earlier on, but the pain in her injured eye had come back with a vengeance. She closed her eyes and tried to ignore the constant throbbing as they drove back to Cambourne. At least the storm had passed. The late afternoon air was now cold, clear and crisp. When they arrived back at the flat, Jack Wilkins insisted on escorting her to the door. She invited him in and apologised for the untidiness of the room. He told her not to worry, he had seen worse, and ushered her to the chair.

He looked at her and smiled sympathetically. 'You do look rough.'

'I feel it.' She fished in her bag for some more painkillers and went to get up.

Wilkins ordered. 'I'll take those, you stay seated.' He went to the kitchen.

Sandra didn't normally like too much fuss, but she felt happy to be pampered for once. She shouted, 'There is some milk in the fridge if you want a coffee.'

'Thanks for the offer but I'd better get back sharpish – DI Everett was looking a bit pressured.' He returned with the tablets and a glass of milk. 'Get those down you.'

Sandra swallowed the tablets and closed her eyes. 'Thanks.'

'Martin Everett will be real proud of what you did today.'

Sandra opened her one good eye. 'Do you think?'

Wilkins nodded. 'Really heroic, and he would be right.' For one brief second they looked at each other affectionately. 'We'll see how you are tomorrow. You might need a day off.'

Sandra dismissed him with a wave of her hand. 'I'll be fine – mind you, I'll need someone to come and pick me up.'

Jack Wilkins grinned. 'At your service.'

Sandra closed her eyes once again. 'Thanks, Jack, see you in the morning.'

He closed the door softly as he left the flat.

On the drive back to Helston, he received a radio message from HQ that Luke Sadler had been trying to get in touch with him. In all the excitement and drama of the events which had unfolded that afternoon, he'd forgotten all about Daniel Felton. He rang Luke's number.

Luke answered immediately; he sounded anxious. 'Hello.'

'Hello, Mr Sadler, Sergeant Wilkins here.'

'Hello, Sergeant, I've been trying to get hold of you all afternoon. I heard that you'd been called away urgently – did it have anything to do with Daniel?'

'It did, but don't worry, Daniel is OK.'

'Thank God for that. There's been no way I can reach him, I've been worried sick.'

'Basically, those two men you told us about somehow managed to track him down.'

'I think I know how. My car was in for a service today

and the mechanic discovered a tracking device hidden in the wheel arch.'

'That would be it then.'

'So can you tell me what happened?'

Wilkins chose his words carefully. 'The good news is we managed to save Daniel from a potentially sticky situation; the bad news is there were a couple of fatalities, sadly one of them being the man who helped Daniel. It's complicated, so the press have not been told too much at present. You'll know a bit more when it's all made public.'

'Would it be possible for you to get Daniel to ring me?'

Wilkins looked at the time. It was coming up to six in the evening. It would mean driving past Helston and on to Tregarris. He was just about to answer in the negative when Luke spoke again.

'Please, I really would appreciate it.'

There was a hint of desperation in Luke's voice. Wilkins felt himself weaken. What was another thirty minutes on his journey? 'OK, I'll see if I can track him down.'

'Thanks, Sergeant.'

He quickly radioed in a message to HQ, giving them the reason for his delayed return.

The Chough was in darkness when Wilkins arrived at the cottage and parked his car. Daniel's Fiat was parked outside but there were no signs of life inside. He pulled on the bell rope outside the door. The reverberations lingered mournfully in the cold night air, but there was no answer. Thinking there was only one likely place where Daniel would possibly spend his time on such a night, he decided to walk along to the Jolly Pirate and take a look. The pub was even livelier than normal for a Thursday night, as not surprisingly there had been plenty of excitement generated by the afternoon's events. Many curious faces turned to stare as the uniformed Jack Wilkins entered the pub. Doing his best to look impervious to the attention, Wilkins' eyes scanned the bar for Daniel. He was nowhere to be seen. He spotted the publican and approached him. 'Hello again, Mr Turner, have you seen the young man from the Chough, Daniel Felton, in here tonight?'

Reg looked relieved. 'So he wasn't one of the men that went off the cliff this afternoon, I'm so glad to hear that.'

Wilkins reassured him on that point. 'No, Mr Turner, if that is the rumour, I can officially confirm right now that there is no truth in it. But I take it from that you haven't seen him?'

'No, not a sign of him.'

'If he does come in here tonight, can you ask him to ring his cousin?'

'No problem.'

Wilkins suddenly remembered. 'Have you fixed your backdoor yet?'

Reg grinned genially. 'It's all sorted, Sergeant.'

Wilkins gestured around the busy bar. 'If your custom carries on like this, you'll soon get your money back.'

Reg shook his head ruefully. 'Unfortunately it looks like dead bodies are good for business. It's a strange world.'

Wilkins had to agree. 'It sure is.'

As Jack Wilkins walked back to his car, he was in a bit of a dilemma. Daniel was nowhere to be found, but he felt it was a little too early to start getting worried. Daniel would have been frightened out of his wits when the two heavies turned up and had probably decided to lie low until the coast was clear. He certainly did not want to needlessly alarm his cousin. Luke Sadler sounded worried enough already. He decided to pass on the news of Daniel's absence to Martin Everett when he got back. It would be for his boss to decide if and when the time was right to employ the Cornwall Search and Rescue Team once more.

*

Daniel felt himself stumble for the umpteenth time. He was shaking and confused. He vaguely remembered running inland across the fields, but with the moon casting its mysterious shadows, he had become totally disorientated, losing all sense of time and place. He had completely forgotten what he was running from. He had no idea where he was running to. Why was he even running? At that moment he didn't have a clue. His eyes were struggling to focus as he stared into the murky gloom. Thirty yards ahead of him loomed a dark shape. It was a structure of some kind. He staggered awkwardly towards it, hardly able to lift his feet. The building seemed to have a wall missing. He fell inside. It was a derelict old barn. He slowly crawled towards the corner and rolled into a ball. He felt safe here. No one could touch him. He was shivering and his eyes felt heavy. There was what looked like an old sheet of tarpaulin lying nearby. He pulled it over him and fell asleep within seconds.

*

It was just approaching midnight when Jack Wilkins returned to the Chough cottage accompanied by two officers. It had been agreed that he should return to Tregarris one more time after discussing Daniel's disappearance with DI Everett earlier that evening. As before, the cottage looked dark and empty, with Daniel's car still parked outside. Once more there was no response from inside after Wilkins rang the bell. He looked up at the upstairs windows. Of course there was a chance that Daniel was hiding inside. He was reluctant but it could not be helped. He signalled for one of the officers to break the lock on the front door. There was a loud crack before the officer pushed open the door and entered. Wilkins followed him in and quickly searched for the light switch. As the light flooded the hallway he shouted Daniel's name, before mounting the small staircase that led to the bedrooms. After a quick search, it was obvious that Daniel had not returned to the cottage since his encounter with the two men earlier that day. Returning downstairs, he took one more look around. His eyes fell upon the large grandfather clock, its hands stopped at three o'clock. He suddenly felt a cold shudder, as if someone had poured cold water down his neck. He felt what could only be described as morbid anxiety beginning to creep over him. Fortunately he did not have time to dwell on this as he was soon joined by the two officers and they exited the cottage together.

After a swift makeshift repair to secure the front door, the three of them walked up to the coastal path and had a quick scan left and right. A cold, biting breeze was gusting in from the moonlit coastline. It was not a night to be spent outdoors. Wilkins called out Daniel's name and listened, but the only sound to be heard was the receding echoes of his own voice. When they got back to the car, he radioed in to DI Everett to inform him of Daniel's continued disappearance. Unfortunately it now looked to be another job for the search and rescue team.

On the drive back to Helston, Jack Wilkins was a little distracted in his thoughts. He was feeling strangely unsettled and he realised that it was not just his concern for Daniel Felton that had left him with a bad feeling. There was something else. He could not begin to explain it, but he had been disturbed by something in the atmosphere back at the empty cottage. He glanced at his wristwatch. It was now well into the early hours. It did not look like he would be getting any sleep tonight.

TEN

LOST AND FOUND

Captain Mike Townsend of the Police Air Operations Unit was nearing the end of his four-hour shift. The morning light was beginning to break through as he circled his yellow and blue liveried helicopter one more time. For the majority of that early morning, he had been sweeping the coastline where the last known sighting of someone matching Daniel Felton's description had been reported. Disappointingly his thermal imaging cameras had so far failed to detect anything significant and his search had proved fruitless. On his last sweep he had decided to widen his search by about a half a mile inland.

Nearing the end of his circle, he was just about to turn around and head back to Exeter HQ, when he caught sight of an old isolated outbuilding. He swept in to obtain a better view. On closer inspection it appeared to be the remains of a disused barn, but more crucially, his thermal imaging was definitely picking something up. With his well-honed instincts telling him he had found something significant, he radioed in to police HQ.

Down below in the barn, Daniel was drifting in and out of consciousness. He may have been dimly aware of the drone of the helicopter circling above him, but as regards anything else he was totally oblivious. For the severe cold he had endured overnight had rendered him incapable of any logical thought.

*

Reg Turner struggled to suppress a yawn as he pulled open the heavy curtain that covered his windows in the bar area. The morning light flooded the room and hurt his eyes. He had not had a good night. What with the pub burglary and the drama of the cliff deaths from the day before, he felt he was getting more excitement than was probably good for him. It had not helped that he had been kept awake in the early hours by the sound of a helicopter continually circling overhead. He sincerely hoped they were not still searching for the young man from the Chough cottage. In the short time he had known Daniel he had taken a bit of a shine to him. Worryingly, the police sergeant who had come into the pub last night looking for him had not been too reassuring.

As he turned to walk back to the bar, he felt his foot come into contact with an object that sped across the floor. He bent down and picked it up. It was a distinctively hooked Dupont cigarette lighter in black and chrome. It must have been lying on the floor behind the curtain. It was an expensive-looking item. Thinking that the owner could well return to the pub in search of it, he placed it in the drawer behind the bar.

*

Joe Blades was beginning to feel anxious. He had tried to ring Vince several times from his office in Soho, but he was not picking up. He had not heard from him since yesterday morning – it was now approaching midday. It was not like him to fail to report in. Something was wrong. He instinctively started to clear his desk. It suddenly seemed like a good idea for him to disappear for a few months. He methodically started to fill his briefcase with documents relating to his dubious practices. After emptying all the drawers, he went over to the safe and calmly tapped in the combination. It sprung open to reveal thousands of pounds, neatly stacked in varying denominations secured by elastic bands. Moving quickly and efficiently, he proceeded to load the money into a large Gladstone bag made of calfskin leather. He could think of a couple of options for his bolthole; it would not be the first time he'd had to leave London in a hurry. Before leaving the office, he went over to a small mirror hanging on the wall and meticulously straightened his tie. He then picked up the bag and briefcase and descended the short flight of stairs that led to the front door.

Stepping out into Beak Street, he turned to lock the door. It was then he heard a voice behind him. 'Going somewhere nice, Mr Blades?'

He turned around to be confronted by three constables from the Metropolitan Police. The game was obviously up.

He dropped his bag on the floor and let out a small sigh of resignation. In that moment Joe Blades realised that for the foreseeable future there was only one place where he was heading; and by no stretch of the imagination could it be described as nice.

*

Reg Turner poked his head into the pub kitchen. It was just approaching midday and Head Chef Jed Harris looked hard-pressed. He was busy sorting out a delivery of fresh prawns and crab that were on the menu for that evening. Reg was looking to have a word with the new kitchen porter, George Rosie. He had not liked what he had heard from Jed regarding his latest recruit's attitude. His plan was to give him a pep talk and allow him one more chance.

'Hello, Jed, is young George about? After our conversation the other day, I was hoping to have that chat with him.'

Jed pulled a face. 'You'll be lucky. I've not seen him since yesterday lunchtime. It's not good enough, Ted, he'll have to go.'

Reg was disappointed. 'That bad, is it?'

Jed sounded annoyed. 'Worse than bad, he's been a complete waste of space these last two days. His head is somewhere else. Yesterday he spent most of the time asking for matches to light his cigs and moaning about his lost lighter.'

Reg could not help showing his surprise. So it looked like the fancy lighter he had found in the bar could have belonged to Rosie. Thinking about the location where it was found, he would have put money on it belonging to a customer. He wanted to make sure. 'I think I just might be able to help him with that. Do you know what his lighter looked like?'

Jed did not hesitate. 'Yeah, it's one of those flash ones with the hook on.'

A sudden upsetting realisation began to occur to Reg. 'Let him know that I want to see him when he comes in, Jed.'

Jed gave an empty laugh. '*If* he comes in.'

Reg went back to the bar and retrieved the lighter from the drawer. He looked at it thoughtfully. Could it be that George Rosie had dropped it when hiding behind the curtain on the night of the burglary? Waiting for him to turn his back before making a quick getaway? He thought of the recent spate of discrepancies in the till money. It was a definite possibility. He certainly would have had ample opportunity to damage the bolt on the backdoor in preparation for his nocturnal visit. Of course, there could be a perfectly good explanation and Rosie could be completely innocent. Reg thought it would be interesting to hear what the young man had to say when he finally confronted him with the lighter. Looking troubled, he slipped the lighter in his pocket, before opening the pub doors for the lunchtime session.

*

'Pug, will you quit making that horrible noise? You sound like a stuck pig.'

George Rosie was talking to Jenna in the churchyard. She was crying. Along with Ricky Carlyon, they had agreed to meet up after Jenna had threatened to tell the police the truth.

She looked at him accusingly. 'You promised you would be my boyfriend if I told the police what you wanted… you were lying.'

Rosie struggled to keep a smirk off his face. 'Believe me, I would love to go out with you, Pug, but there's too much going on.'

Jenna replied angrily, 'Will you stop calling me Pug!'

Rosie laughed. 'It's only a term of affection.' He put his arm around her. 'Do you want me to write you one of my poems? Would you like that?'

'I just want you to do what you promised, that's all.'

'I'm sorry, Pug, it's just not the right time.'

Jenna realised that there was never going to be a right time; he had taken her for a fool. She started to sob once more.

Rosie took a box of matches from his pocket and lit another cigarette. He wished he knew where he had left that damned lighter. He took a deep drag and glowered at Ricky Carlyon. 'Why have you got such a long face?'

Carlyon scowled back at him. 'I don't like the way you talk to her.'

Rosie looked at him with contempt. 'You soft tosser.' He reached into his pocket and pulled out a small bag of white powder. 'Look what I've got. I'll be able to write some great poetry with this stuff.'

Carlyon looked a little shocked. 'Is that what I think it is?'

Rosie grinned. 'It's hallucinogenic, very expensive, should make me very creative.'

'Where did you get it?'

'Dealer I know.'

Carlyon looked disgusted. 'Have you been dipping into Reg Turner's till again?'

Rosie shrugged. 'What of it?'

Ricky Carlyon stood up. 'You're going too far, George. I was going to tell you that the police were round my house yesterday. They suspect I might have something to do with the harassment of the Emmet in Chough cottage.'

Rosie laughed in his face. 'You have!'

'Well, no more, I'm out of it.'

Rosie sneered. 'That's the trouble with you, Carlyon, you're a lightweight. You've got no spunk. Just you remember you're in it with me, right up to your neck. There's no walking away.'

Ricky snapped back. 'It wasn't me that tortured and kicked that drifter.'

Rosie stood up and faced him, his expression and manner turning ugly. 'You seem to forget that you were with me, Carlyon. That makes you as guilty as I am.'

Ricky felt his temper rising. 'You're not pinning that one on me – I tried to stop you.'

Rosie stood in front of him provocatively and pushed Ricky's chest. 'Did you? I can't say I remember that.'

In an instant, the two young men launched themselves at each other ferociously with fists clenched. Jenna screamed for them to stop but could only look on helplessly. The conflict that followed was fast and furious, with punches being given and received with aggressive vigour. With neither of them being prepared to give ground, the burlier George Rosie began to slowly gain the advantage. The end when it came was both brutal and efficient. Two solid punches to the jaw brought Ricky Carlyon to his knees. It was then that Rosie proceeded to put the boot in.

*

Sarah Thomson was coming to the end of her routine walk along the coastal path. Because a part of the path had been closed, she was taking the route across the fields that took her past the church for the last section back to Tregarris. She shook her head slowly and tutted to herself. The detour was to do with all this business with the tragic deaths of the two men. Since she had discovered the body of the murdered Duncan Fraser the week previous, the usually quiet village of Tregarris had been abuzz with the incident and had already gained some local notoriety. This latest episode with the two men perishing at the bottom of the cliffs had taken things one step further, with it even being reported on the lunchtime bulletins of BBC and Sky News. If she was being totally honest with herself, there was a part of her that was secretly enjoying all the excitement.

She had just closed the gate that led into the churchyard, when she heard a girl's voice shouting. It was loud and it was urgent. 'Stop it, George, stop it!'

Sarah Thomson was confronted by the sight of a young man kicking out savagely at someone who was on the floor. She shouted out instinctively for the man to stop. He ceased kicking and looked up, caught by surprise at the interruption. Before Sarah could say anything else, he was on his heels and away down the lane that led to the village. The girl, whom Sarah instantly recognised as someone she had seen frequently in Tregarris, immediately run after him.

When she drew closer to the figure on the ground, she knew instantly that it was young Ricky Carlyon, Elsie's boy. He was lying curled up in a ball and when he heard her voice, he started to sob uncontrollably. Sarah comforted him as best she could, before slowly helping him to his feet. His face was bleeding and badly swollen and he seemed groggy in his responses.

Sarah looked at him compassionately. 'Ricky, I'm not even going to begin to ask what this is all about. Let's just get you home to your mum.'

She led him slowly and unsteadily down the hill to the village.

*

It was getting on for mid-afternoon as Jack Wilkins drove towards Sandra Kent's flat in Cambourne. Sandra had rung Helston HQ to say she felt well enough to come back in and he had volunteered to go and pick her up. The early morning search for Daniel Felton had ensured a busy start to the day and he'd hardly had any sleep in the last twenty-four hours. After locating Daniel's whereabouts, the rescue team had immediately transported him to hospital. He sincerely hoped the poor lad would pull through OK. It had certainly not been an easy phone call to Luke Sadler. Having to tell him that his cousin had been rushed to hospital after he had spent the night exposed in a derelict barn took some explaining.

As he pulled up outside Sandra's flat, the November sun was shining brightly and the air was crisp. She was already standing there waiting, a pair of dark glasses her only concession to her eye injury.

She smiled as she got in the car. 'Thanks for the lift.'

Wilkins grinned back. 'All part of the service.' It felt good to be back in her company. 'How's the eye?'

Sandra removed her glasses and examined it in the rear mirror. 'Much improved, though probably sensible to wear the shades.'

'It makes you look a cool dude.'

Sandra laughed a little self-consciously. Wilkins went on to bring her up to speed on Daniel Felton.

After he had finished, Sandra looked a little concerned. 'Will he be OK?'

'Too early to say. He was in a pretty bad way.'

'Have you told his cousin?'

Wilkins grimaced as he nodded. 'Not the most pleasant duty I've performed today. He's coming down from London tomorrow. Let's hope he gets some good news.'

There was a brief, sombre silence before Wilkins changed the subject. 'You will be pleased to know that your black eye was not in vain. Everett got Vince Mitchell to snitch on his boss. Turns out it was a dude called Joe Blades who worked out of Soho. He was not exactly unknown to Scotland Yard, but until now he has always been a slippery eel to catch.' He offered Sandra his hand for a high five.

She slapped it enthusiastically. 'My eye is feeling better by the second.'

A phone call came in from Helston HQ informing them that Elsie Carlyon had rung in saying she had some important information regarding Duncan Fraser.

Wilkins looked across at Sandra. 'Sounds interesting – feel up to another trip to Tregarris?'

Kent nodded vigorously. 'You bet.'

Jack Wilkins put his foot down on the accelerator.

*

Some thirty minutes later, both Wilkins and Kent were sitting in Elsie Carlyon's small sitting room once more. Elsie, who looked like she had been crying, was seated next to Ricky on the sofa. Sarah Thomson was making herself busy in the tiny kitchenette area, having already made a statement of what she had witnessed. Even though Elsie had attended to his facial injuries, Ricky Carlyon looked a sorry sight. His features were severely battered, his body language submissive. He looked like he had given up.

With a deeply concerned expression, Elsie spoke to Ricky. 'I want you to tell them everything you know, Ricky, everything you have told me.'

Ricky looked across at Sergeant Wilkins and PC Kent and mumbled, 'I know who killed the drifter.'

Sandra Kent got out her pen and notebook. 'In your own time, Ricky.'

Ricky swallowed hard. 'It's the same Bleddy Tuss I had the scrap with today. He lives in Bosnick and his name is George Rosie.'

Sandra wrote the detail down. 'Can you tell us how you come to know it was him that attacked Duncan Fraser?'

He put his hands to his face. 'Because I was there with him.'

Jack Wilkins leant forward. 'Probably best if you start at the beginning, Ricky.'

'I met him through Jenna Truscott. I've known her since I was a kid.'

Sandra coaxed him gently. 'We know Jenna. I take it she was the girl that Miss Thomson saw run away today?'

'Yeah, he'd offered her a lift at the bus stop a couple of months ago, and she's been totally taken in by George ever since – she'd follow him anywhere, poor kid. She loves to hear him reading out his poems. He said he wrote them especially for her.' Carlyon sounded exasperated. 'She couldn't see that he was totally stringing her along. He even calls her Pug for Christ's sake.'

'Pug?'

'As in Pug ugly.'

Sandra Kent could not help shaking her head. 'Sounds a real charmer.'

Carlyon went on. 'She introduced me to him outside the Pirate a few months back. He seemed a good bloke. He had even got Reg Turner to give him a job in the pub. Oh, he can be a right charmer when he wants to be. He used to smuggle me out free bottles of Proper Job from the fridge in the pub kitchen.'

Wilkins pointed out, 'So he was thieving.'

Carlyon looked expressionless. 'Suppose he was.'

'There's no suppose about it. Would I also be right in

thinking that he has been dipping into Mr Turner's till on a regular basis?'

There was no hesitation from Carlyon. 'Yeah.'

'So what happened on the night Duncan Fraser died?'

'I can see now that all the free booze was about getting me drunk and winding me up about the incomers. I had told him about the disappointment with the Chough cottage and how Mum felt we were being pushed out. He just seemed to find it all very amusing. From then on he would be in my ear at every opportunity, needling me about the Emmets. When the incomer turned up at the cottage, he couldn't wait to cause some trouble. On that particular night I'd drunk a lot. When he said we should follow the fella back to the cottage and shout some abuse it seemed like a good idea. But afterwards George wanted to go further. He gave me his car key and pointed to the Fiat parked outside the cottage. Think of your mum, he said.'

'I take it you then keyed the car?'

Carlyon glanced agitatedly at his mum. 'Yeah.'

'So what happened then?'

The drifter came walking by, heading for the coastal path. I had seen him before, so I was not surprised when he started shouting abuse at us. The poor man was not right in the head. I shouted back at him and we followed him to the coastal path. It seemed a good laugh. But then George started smacking him around the head. I told him to stop but he was obviously enjoying it. He had a strange look on his face. He then started kicking the man till he fell to the ground.'

Carlyon paused for a few seconds, obviously disturbed

and upset at the memory. 'He kicked him again on the floor and then started burning him with his cigarette. I begged him to stop, but it was as if I wasn't there. He was in his own little twisted world.'

'Was Duncan Fraser still conscious?'

'Yeah, he was still moaning and shouting when we left him. Rosie took Fraser's banjo and rucksack with him. I couldn't believe he could be so wicked. From that point on I wanted to get away from George and never see him again, but then we heard that the drifter was found dead the next morning. I wanted to go straight to the police, but Rosie kept reminding me that I was as guilty as he was because I never stopped him. I wanted nothing more to do with it, but he said that if I helped him dispose of the rucksack he would leave me alone. But I should have known he was lying. He was never going to let me walk away. It was only afterwards that I found out about his moronic plan to frame the Emmet by getting poor Jenna to lie to the police. The poor kid believed him when he promised he would be her boyfriend and told her she would get the reward money. It was Jenna that told me he was continuing to harass and shout abuse at the incomer from the top of the hill. She said he told her he was doing it because he enjoyed the thought that I might get the blame.'

There was a sombre silence before Sandra Kent asked, 'Have you got George Rosie's address?'

Carlyon winced with pain as he shifted his position on the chair. 'I only know it's the last building in a row of old mining cottages in Bosnick. He rents a room there.'

'We'll find it. What car does he drive?'

'He's got a battered old Morris. It's usually caked in mud but I think the colour's dark blue.'

Jack Wilkins turned to Elsie Carlyon. 'Obviously you realise the seriousness of these revelations, Mrs Carlyon. At some point we will require Ricky to come into Helston Police Station and make a formal statement.' He gave a quick glance towards Ricky. 'So don't even think of going anywhere in the next few days.' He turned back to Elsie. 'I can tell you now, Ricky will be charged with manslaughter and it's likely he will serve a sentence. Do you understand?'

Elsie Carlyon's lower lip trembled. 'Do you know how long he could be away for?'

'It's difficult to say for sure. Ricky's confession and the fact he has no criminal record could go in his favour, but if the worst happens and George Rosie successfully contests his version of events, we could be talking a long sentence under joint enterprise.'

Fighting back the tears, Elsie put her arm around Ricky and showed a brave face. 'The fact is, Ricky knows he has done wrong, and because of that we should be prepared to accept the consequences together.'

Wilkins looked back at Ricky Carlyon. 'In the meantime, it's probably a good idea to get those injuries checked out with your doctor.'

Elsie pulled Ricky closer. 'We'll get it sorted, Sergeant.'

As Wilkins and Kent left the house they had plenty to think about. If Ricky Carlyon was telling the truth about George Rosie, it sounded like they could be dealing with someone who was bordering on psychopathic. Either way it sounded like he was one nasty piece of work.

After swiftly establishing with Reg Turner in the Jolly

Pirate that George Rosie had not turned up for work that day, Wilkins and Kent stopped by at Jenna Truscott's house. Unsurprisingly, she was not at home. According to her stepfather, he had not seen her since she had left the house that morning. After radioing in to Helston HQ informing them to put out a lookout for a battered old Morris and requesting some backup, they made their way towards Bosnick.

The November evening was drawing in fast when they finally pulled up outside the small row of white cottages. There was a downstairs light glowing in the end cottage, but no sign of Rosie's Morris outside. Wilkins did think about knocking before the backup arrived but thought better of it. If everything he had heard so far about Rosie was true, it was probably wise to be cautious. After about ten minutes the patrol car turned up and they were joined by two other officers. The four of them approached the front door. After a short wait the door was opened by a small man in his mid-forties.

Wilkins guessed he was the landlord. 'Do you have a George Rosie staying here?'

The man looked a little alarmed. 'I do. Why, what's he been up to?'

'I take it he's not in?'

'No, he left with that girl who comes pestering about an hour ago.'

'Can we see his room?'

'Sure you can.' He stepped aside and followed them up the small staircase. He continued to talk. 'I thought he'd been in trouble. He looked like he'd been fighting; he had a fat lip. It's the door just in front of you.'

They opened it. The room in front of them was dank and musty, with the single light bulb barely throwing enough light to illuminate the far corners. Papers and books were strewn across the floor.

Sandra Kent gave a low whistle. She wasn't normally fazed by untidiness, but this was something else. She bent and picked up a couple of the books: *Sons and Lovers*, *The Catcher in the Rye*. She showed them to Jack Wilkins. 'Obviously likes a good novel.'

Wilkins was unimpressed. 'Bit heavy for me, I prefer autobiographies.'

Sandra also noticed there were a number of books with poetry anthologies among the sheets of paper. The paper sheets appeared to be full of what looked like half-finished poems and song lyrics. In the main, the verse seemed to be about love and loss, but there were some where the subject matter appeared to be very dark indeed. She handed a couple over to Jack Wilkins. After giving them a quick scan, he shook his head slowly in disbelief. They were obviously dealing with an individual who was very seriously damaged. They were just about to leave when one of the officers called him over. He was crouching down by the side of the bed. There was a small paper bag on the floor with some traces of crystallised white powder strewn across the carpet.

Wilkins bent down to take a look. 'Looks like some heady stuff. It doesn't look like coke.'

Sandra handed him a small evidence bag before enquiring, 'DMT?'

'I'd put money on it.' He stood up and turned to the

landlord, who was standing outside the room. 'How long has he stayed here?'

'About three months.'

'Is he a good tenant?'

'He always pays his rent if that's what you mean.'

'How do you find him as a person?'

'Most of the time he can seem quite normal and even friendly, but...' The landlord hesitated.

Wilkins coaxed him. 'Go on.'

'I hear him talking to himself in the room, sometimes quite loudly.'

'Anything else?'

'As I say, he can be very chatty; other times he can look right through you and even be downright rude. I can never make him out.'

'Did he say where he was going when he left earlier?'

'No, nothing. He just walked straight past me with that funny little girl that follows him around.'

Sandra handed him her contact number. 'If he returns, don't say anything to him but inform us straight away.'

The man looked a little alarmed. 'Is he dangerous?'

Sandra gave Jack Wilkins a quick glance before she answered, 'Probably best if you just do as we say, Mr...?

'Saunders, Don Saunders.'

Before returning to Helston HQ, Jack Wilkins thought it might be a good idea to drive back to Tregarris to take one more look around.

Sandra Kent sat in the passenger seat, gazing out at the dark silhouetted hedges that lined the road back to Tregarris. It was not comforting to think that Jenna Truscott was out there somewhere, alone with Rosie. She wanted some reassurance from Jack Wilkins. 'Where do you think they've gone?'

Wilkins changed down to third gear as he negotiated a narrow bend, the eyes of a fox momentarily reflecting in his headlights. 'That's a very good question – hopefully not too far away from here.'

'Do you think Jenna is in danger?'

'Unfortunately from all we know so far of George Rosie, I think you would have to say yes.'

They drove on towards Tregarris in thoughtful silence. Then they saw it. It was Sandra Kent that saw it first: a dark shape parked in the layby on a minor approach road that led into the village. Jack Wilkins pulled up a few yards along the road. He recognised the area. It was the road at the top of the winding lane that led up from the Jolly Pirate. From where they were sitting, the vehicle appeared to be empty. It definitely matched the description of George Rosie's Morris.

Both of them detached their ASP batons and torches from their belts before leaving the car. The country road was dark and deserted as they walked towards the Morris cautiously. They peered through the windows. There was nobody inside. Wilkins tried opening the door on the driver's side. It was unlocked. He quickly scanned the interior, but apart from some discarded food packaging and a few sweet wrappers, there was nothing to see. He walked to the back of the car and opened the boot. The only item inside was a grimy old muslin sack. It was empty.

The stillness of the evening was suddenly broken by the sound of the Tregarris church bells ringing in the distance. Sandra Kent looked at her watch. It was ten minutes past ten. She looked puzzled. 'Why are the church bells ringing?' Jack Wilkins was just about to answer when Sandra's phone went off.

It was Jenna Truscott; she sounded distressed. 'Please help, it's George. There's something wrong – he's not right in the head.'

'Where are you, Jenna?'

'In the churchyard, George is ringing the bells. He's been taking stuff. I'm scared of what he might do.'

'We'll be there in a minute, Jenna, try to stay calm.'

Jack Wilkins gave Sandra a knowing look as she rang off. 'Don't tell me, it's Rosie that's ringing the bells.'

She gave a quick nod of confirmation before they ran back to the patrol car.

Just minutes later they were hurriedly ascending the hill that led up to the church. They had called for backup and a nearby patrol car was on its way. By the time they had reached the churchyard, the reverberating chimes of the church bells had been replaced by another sound that carried hauntingly on the evening air. It was the soft, melodious strumming of a banjo. They looked up towards the roof of the church. The evening was cold and cloudless, with the moonlight vividly illuminating the top of the bell tower. There they clearly saw the profile of George Rosie, Duncan Fraser's banjo in his hands, appearing totally oblivious to their presence as he straddled the parapet. Jenna Truscott was sitting on a gravestone just a few yards away. She was quietly sobbing. Sandra Kent went over to comfort her.

Wilkins cupped his hands and shouted up to George

Rosie, 'George, this is the police. We advise you to come down immediately for your own safety.'

There was no answer from him. His only response seemed to be a more strident, rhythmic strumming of the banjo. As two other officers arrived in the churchyard, Wilkins called out to Sandra, 'I'm going up there to see if we can talk him down.' He signalled for the two officers to follow him. Just as they were about to enter the church doorway, Wilkins paused briefly at the bottom of the steps and listened. Something had changed. The repeated strumming of the banjo had stopped. For a few brief moments the only sound he could hear was the distant surf breaking on the rocks below. Then out of the blue, the jolting shock of a loud bang rang out across the churchyard like a small explosion. Sadly it was a sound that Jack Wilkins had heard far too often in his relatively short police career. It was the sickening noise of bones cracking on unyielding flagstone. George Rosie had thrown himself off the bell tower.

*

It was fast approaching midday on the Saturday morning in the Royal Cornwall Hospital in Truro. Daniel Felton was lying on a bed in the general ward gently dozing. He had been in a bad way when the rescue services had found him semi-conscious in the derelict barn. He had immediately been put on oxygen before being transported to the hospital as an emergency case. Once admitted, he had been found to be suffering from severe hyperthermia and a low heart rate. The medics had wasted no time in warming his blood intravenously.

Now, twenty-four hours later, he had thankfully made a full recovery and was currently under observation. He stirred and turned over in his sleep. As he drifted once more into a pleasurable light doze, he began to enjoy a beautiful dream. He was somewhere on the Cornish coastal path. The sun felt warm on his face under a vivid blue sky, the sea a glittering turquoise. In the far distance he could make out what looked like a large marquis, its vivid red and white colouring shimmering attractively in the bright sunlight. He tried walking towards it, but it did not seem to be getting any closer. He became vaguely aware of someone calling his name repeatedly.

He awoke and opened his eyes to be greeted by three smiling and mightily relieved faces. It was Luke, Kate and Lauren. It was a cheerful sight.

Daniel immediately turned to Lauren. 'You did believe me, didn't you?'

She was quick to give him a reassuring hug. 'Of course I did, I just needed to think things through, that's all.'

Daniel found it difficult to contain his elation. 'I'm so glad you're here, I really thought you had given up on me.'

Lauren smiled but she sounded serious. 'I won't deny that there have been moments when I thought about it.' She moved closer and squeezed his hand. 'But the good news for you is I think you're worth the effort. I've spoken to your mum and dad by the way, and not surprisingly they agree.'

Daniel looked a little perturbed. 'Have you told them everything?'

'Not everything, but just enough – bottom line is we think it's time for you to come home.'

Daniel turned to Luke. 'What about the two men?'

Luke smiled. 'Don't worry, fella, it's all sorted. We've come straight here from the Helston Police Station. Sergeant Wilkins has told us all about it.'

It was all coming back to Daniel. 'There was another man, he was trying to help.'

Luke spoke soothingly. 'All in good time, Daniel, all in good time.'

Kate added, 'In the meantime we've got some big plans for you, Daniel, so be sure to get yourself fit and well.'

Daniel looked back towards Lauren, her expression full of loving concern. He was struggling to take it all in, but in that moment of one thing he was certain.

He could not remember the last time he had felt so happy.

*

Back at Helston HQ, DI Everett was discussing George Rosie with Jack Wilkins and Sandra Kent. Though Martin Everett had not been left totally untouched by the tragic loss of his old Met colleague Mark Reid, the arrest of Joe Blades and the successful conclusion to the Duncan Fraser case had left him in a good mood. He had just received the latest medical update on Rosie's condition from the Royal Cornwall.

'Doctors say he has two broken legs and a fractured pelvis, also confirm he was full of chemicals. He must have been as high as a kite when he jumped. For all that, they're cautiously optimistic he'll recover, but it's going to be a long haul.'

Jack Wilkins remarked, 'That's something, I suppose.'

Everett did not sound totally convinced. 'I'm not so sure about that. His physical injuries will probably eventually heal, but as for his mental state, your guess is as good as mine.'

Sandra thought back to some of the dark and macabre prose she had read on the sheets of paper back in his room. 'Yes, going by his poetry, whatever was going on between his ears is going to take a whole lot longer to fathom.'

Wilkins nodded in agreement. 'He was certainly no Wordsworth, that's for sure.'

Everett was taking another look at his notes. 'It seems Rosie originally lived in Penzance. I suppose it comes as no surprise that his dad also had a history of mental illness and substance abuse before passing away two years ago.'

Wilkins was not surprised. 'Psychosis does tend to run in families: I've seen it far too often. What do you think will happen with young Carlyon?'

'Probably anything from about six months to two years at the most – it will teach him a lesson for being such a foolish boy.'

Wilkins thought of Carlyon's poor old mum Elsie and shook his head. 'We live and learn, I guess.'

Sandra Kent asked, 'What about the girl?'

Everett was definite with his answer. 'No charges pressed – the poor girl looks like she has had more than enough to put up with.'

Both Kent and Wilkins gave a nod of silent approval at Martin Everett's reply.

Everett went over to his desk and picked up Duncan Fraser's banjo. It had been placed there earlier after Jack Wilkins had retrieved it from the bell tower. He gave it a strum. 'I know you would normally have first claim on the banjo, Jack, but would you mind if I have this after the conviction? I'd like to keep it as a souvenir.'

Wilkins grinned. 'It's all yours.'

Everett gave it another strum before remarking, 'At least young Felton is on the mend. Perhaps he and his cousin will have a quieter life from now on.'

Wilkins replied, 'Sadler and Felton are good lads, I wish them well. They just went about things the wrong way.'

Sandra could not help sounding a little smug. 'That was always my feeling.'

Everett gave her a big grin. 'Well, not for the first time, Sandra, your instincts were right on this one. Which reminds me, has the lock on the Chough cottage been properly repaired yet?'

She smiled back at him. 'It's all under control, sir, being repaired as we speak.'

Everett liked the answer. 'By the way, I would like to congratulate you both for some great work over the last few days. The two of you make a terrific team.'

Both Wilkins and Sandra Kent looked a little embarrassed at the compliment before catching each other's eye. In that brief moment their eyes locked and lingered. Again Jack Wilkins felt that connection. Surely she had felt it too. Was it possible that just maybe, there really was a chance? One thing he knew for sure: he would never know unless he found the courage to ask her.

Maybe tomorrow?

SIX MONTHS LATER

Daniel managed to fit in a quick bite of his Subway sandwich before making his next call. Not for the first time, Sadler's Estate Agents seemed to be in the forefront of the latest property boom. It had been Kate's idea to introduce him to the wonderful world of verbal offers, transfer deeds, seller's instructions, home buyers reports and land certificates. Much to his delighted surprise, he was relishing every minute of it.

After returning to London emotionally bruised and fragile, Luke had immediately arranged for him to have some counselling sessions. Giving some further thought to his unemployed status, Luke and Kate had decided to offer him a job for a trial period in one of the Sadler offices. Though it was an offer of pragmatic kindness, Luke had left him in no doubt that he was presenting an opportunity that he must take with both hands. At first he had felt doubtful that he could make a decent fist of it, worried that he would let them down. It had been Lauren who had convinced him to give it his best shot. When she had spoken to him optimistically and earnestly of their planned future together, there was really only one decision to make. It had meant going back home to live with his parents in the short term, but that was a small price to pay.

Kate had agreed to be his mentor in the first few months and he had taken full advantage of it, soaking up her knowledge and expertise like a sponge. For the first time, he felt his life had a structure and direction. He realised he'd had a lucky escape. Along with his parents, Luke, Kate and Lauren had given him a solid foundation on which he could now rebuild his life. Without them, there was no doubt he would have gone under. Even now it frightened him to think of how easily he had fallen: the unforgiving black pit into which his life had so alarmingly descended.

After finishing his call, Kate, who was sat opposite, told him that Luke was on the line. He was phoning from his other Hoxton office.

'Hi, Dan, how's it going?'

'All going well so far. Kate is keeping a close eye on me.'

'She's telling me you have it all under control.'

'I try to please. She's trusted me with a couple of triple property chains, so I must be doing something right.'

'Glad to hear it. I take it you aren't missing Cornwall?'

Daniel thought back to that dark, horrific time. It seemed like a different life. 'Would it surprise you if I said not really?'

Luke could not help chuckling. 'That reminds me, we have our first holiday guests staying at the Chough... the Carstairs. I wonder how they're getting on?'

'Well, hopefully they are having a more enjoyable time than I did.'

'That probably wouldn't be too difficult. Keep up the good work. Catch you later.'

'Cheers.'

Daniel looked across at Kate. 'Thanks for the good words, Kate.'

She smiled. 'Credit where credit is due, I was only telling him the truth.'

Daniel looked pleased as he picked up the phone to make his next call. Looking at the paperwork in front of him, it looked like a situation that would need some delicate handling. It was a mark of his new-found confidence that he felt in no way daunted at the prospect.

*

Down in Tregarris in the early hours of the morning, Jim Carstairs woke up with a slight start. He felt he had been dreaming but none of it had made any sense. He shifted his position and moved closer to his wife Julie. It had been a great idea to have a couple of weeks' break in Cornwall. The cottage near the coastal path had proved the ideal base to explore the surrounding areas. Now nearing the end of their first week, his high-stress job as a trader in Canary Wharf seemed a world away. The break had also been good for Julie. He could not remember the last time they had laughed so much together.

He turned over and gradually drifted back into a fitful sleep. He was dreaming he was out on a boat on the ocean, mackerel-fishing. He was pulling in the lines at the rear of the vessel, the fish feeling slimy and twitchy in his hands. He could hear something. There seemed to be a bell sounding on the ocean breeze… his eyes opened wide. He turned over onto his back as Julie stirred and mumbled. The bell had sounded so real. Then he heard it again. It was the bell at the front door. He reached over for his mobile phone. It was three o'clock in the morning. He turned to Julie. 'Did you hear that?' She shifted her position and murmured something incomprehensible. For a brief moment he was in two minds whether to go downstairs and answer the door, but a sense of foreboding that he could not quite explain made him decide against it.

Meanwhile in the doorway outside the cottage, a swirling mist appeared to drift and dance into myriad divergent shapes. Almost imperceptibly, the fluid pattern began to mutate into a discernible bodily form. What finally materialised out of that misty haze did not seem either plausible or possible, but there appeared to be very little doubt… it was Red Robbo.